# Hans Christian Andersen's Fairy Tales

Paper Mill Press Illustrated Classics
is an imprint of Book Depot Inc.
67 Front Street North, Thorold, L2V 1X3 Canada
Printed in China
www.bookdepot.com
Selection, design, arrangement, typesetting, and image reproduction all copyright.
©2022 North Parade Publishing
ISBN: 978-1-77402-219-1

25 24 23 22 • 5 4 3 2 1

# Hans Christian Andersen's
## Fairy Tales

by

# Hans Christian Andersen

with illustrations by

Arthur Rackham, W Heath Robinson & Harry Clarke

# Contents

# Color
# Illustrations

# Introduction

The tales of Hans Christian Andersen have been part of our cultural heritage for over one hundred and fifty years. While the Brothers Grimm were known as collectors of fairy tales and folklore, the Danish author wrote many of his own original stories, some of which have inspired ballets, plays, and films, and have been translated into over one hundred languages.

The son of a cobbler and a washerwoman, Andersen grew up in extreme poverty, but despite his humble beginnings, he went on to achieve fame and recognition in his own lifetime, not only in Europe but in America too, and, after his death, in Asia. He nevertheless remained self-conscious about his background, and cared about what people thought of him—themes which can be found in some of his stories, such as "The Ugly Duckling."

From the poignant beauty of "The Little Mermaid" to the wry humor of "The Emperor's New Clothes," Andersen's classic tales have enchanted and beguiled both children and adults alike across the globe. Filled with magic and wonder, Andersen's stories also offer strong moral messages about flaws such as pride, judging by appearances, and selfishness, and introduce inspirational characters who show resilience, virtue, and courage in the face of adversity. Many of his stories are dark and sinister, and deal with issues such as grief and death, yet others are filled with humor—and every so often you will even find a happy ending!

"Now then, let us begin.
When we are at the end of the story,
we shall know more than we know now . . .
but to begin."

*from* The Snow Queen

# THUMBELINA

There was once a woman who wished very much to have a little child, but she could not obtain her wish. At last she went to a fairy, and said, "I should so very much like to have a little child; can you tell me where I can find one?"

"Oh, that can be easily managed," said the fairy. "Here is a barleycorn of a different kind to those which grow in the farmer's fields, and which the chickens eat; put it into a flowerpot, and see what will happen."

"Thank you," said the woman, and she gave the fairy twelve shillings, which was the price of the barleycorn. Then she went home and planted it, and immediately there grew up a large handsome flower, something like a tulip in appearance, but with its leaves tightly closed as if it were still a bud. "It is a beautiful flower," said the woman, and she kissed the red- and golden-colored leaves, and while she did so the flower opened, and she could see that it was a real tulip. Within the flower, upon the green velvet stamens, sat a very delicate and graceful little maiden. She was scarcely half as long as a thumb, and they gave her the name of "Thumbelina," or Tiny, because she was so small.

A walnut shell, elegantly polished, served her for a cradle; her bed was formed of blue violet leaves, with a rose leaf for a counterpane. Here she slept at night, but during the day she amused herself on a table, where the woman had placed a plateful of water. Around this plate were wreaths of flowers with their stems in the water, and upon it floated a large tulip leaf, which served Tiny for a boat. Here the little maiden sat and rowed herself from side to side, with two oars made of white horsehair. It really was a very pretty sight. Tiny could also sing so softly and sweetly that nothing like her singing had ever before been heard.

One night, while she lay in her pretty bed, a large, ugly, wet toad crept through a broken pane of glass in the window, and leaped right onto the table where Tiny lay sleeping under her rose-leaf quilt. "What a pretty little wife this would make for my son," said the toad, and she took up the walnut shell in which little Tiny lay asleep, and jumped through the window with it into the garden.

In the swampy margin of a broad stream in the garden lived the toad, with her son. He was uglier even than his mother, and when he saw the pretty little maiden in her elegant bed, he could only cry, "Croak, croak, croak."

"Don't speak so loud, or she will wake," said the toad, "and then she might run away, for she is as light as swan's down. We will place her on one of the water-lily leaves out in the stream; it will be like an island to her, she is so light and small, and then she cannot escape; and, while she is away, we will make haste and prepare the stateroom under the marsh, in which you are to live when you are married."

Far out in the stream grew a number of water lilies, with broad green leaves, which seemed to float on the top of the water. The largest of these leaves appeared farther off than the rest, and the old toad swam out to it with the walnut shell, in which little Tiny lay still asleep. The tiny little creature woke very early in the morning, and began to cry bitterly when she found where she was, for she could see nothing but water on every side of the large green leaf, and no way of reaching the land. Meanwhile the old toad was very busy under the marsh, decking her room with rushes and wild yellow flowers, to make it look pretty for her new daughter-in-law. Then she swam out with her ugly son to the leaf on which she had placed poor little Tiny. She wanted to fetch the pretty bed, so that she might put it in the bridal chamber to be ready for her. The old toad bowed low to her in the water, and said, "Here is my son, he will be your husband, and you will live happily in the marsh by the stream."

"Croak, croak, croak," was all her son could say for himself; so the toad took up the elegant little bed, and swam away with it, leaving Tiny all alone on the green leaf, where she sat and wept. She could not bear to think of living with the old toad, and having her ugly son for a husband. The little fishes, who swam about in the water beneath, had seen the toad, and heard what she said, so they lifted their heads above the water to look at the little maiden. As soon as they caught sight of her, they saw she was very pretty, and it made them very sorry to think that she must go and live with the ugly toads. "No, it must never be!"

So they assembled together in the water, around the green stalk which held the leaf on which the little maiden stood, and gnawed it away at the root with their teeth. Then the leaf floated down the stream, carrying Tiny far away out of reach of land.

Tiny sailed past many towns, and the little birds in the bushes saw her, and sang, "What a lovely little creature"; so the leaf swam away with her farther and farther, till it brought her to other lands. A graceful little white butterfly constantly fluttered around her, and at last alighted on the leaf. Tiny pleased him, and she was glad of it, for now the toad could not possibly reach her, and the country through which she sailed was beautiful, and the sun shone upon the water, till it glittered like liquid gold. She took off her girdle and tied one end of it around the butterfly, and the other end of the ribbon she fastened to the leaf, which now glided on much faster than ever, taking little Tiny with it as she stood. Presently a large cockchafer flew by; the moment he caught sight of her, he seized her around her delicate waist with his claws, and flew with her to a tree. The green leaf floated away on the brook, and the butterfly flew with it, for he was fastened to it, and could not get away.

Oh, how frightened little Tiny felt when the cockchafer flew with her to the tree! But especially was she sorry for the beautiful white butterfly which she had fastened to the leaf, for if he could not free himself he would die of hunger. But the cockchafer did not trouble himself at all about the matter. He seated himself by her side on a large green leaf, gave her some honey from the flowers to eat, and told her she was very pretty, though not in the least like a cockchafer. After a time, all the cockchafers turned up their feelers, and said, "She has only two legs! How ugly that looks." "She has no feelers," said another. "Her waist is quite slim. Pooh! She is like a human being."

"Oh! She is ugly," said all the lady cockchafers, although Tiny was very pretty. Then the cockchafer who had run away with her believed all the others when they said she was ugly, and would have nothing more to say to her, and told her she might go where she liked. Then he flew down with her from the tree, and placed her on a daisy, and she wept at the thought that she was so ugly that even the cockchafers would have nothing to say to her. And all the while she was really the loveliest creature that one could imagine, and as tender and delicate as a beautiful rose leaf. During the whole summer poor little Tiny lived quite alone in the wide forest. She wove herself a bed with blades of grass, and hung it up under a broad leaf, to protect herself from the rain. She sucked the honey from the flowers for food, and drank the dew from their leaves every morning.

So passed away the summer and the autumn, and then came the winter—the long, cold winter. All the birds who had sung to her so sweetly were flown away, and the trees and the flowers had withered. The large clover leaf under the shelter of which she had lived was now rolled together and shriveled up—nothing remained but a yellow withered stalk. She felt dreadfully cold, for her clothes were torn, and she was herself so frail and delicate, that poor little Tiny was nearly frozen to death. It began to snow too; and the snowflakes, as they fell upon her, were like a whole shovelful falling upon one of us, for we are tall, but she was only an inch high. Then she wrapped herself up in a dry leaf, but it cracked in the middle and could not keep her warm, and she shivered with cold. Near the wood in which she had been living lay a cornfield, but the corn had been cut a long time; nothing remained but the bare dry stubble standing up out of the frozen ground. It was to her like struggling through a large wood. Oh! How she shivered with the cold. She came at last to the door of a field mouse, who had a little den under the corn stubble. There dwelt the field mouse in warmth and comfort, with a whole roomful of corn, a kitchen, and a beautiful dining room. Poor little Tiny stood before the door just like a little beggar-girl, and begged for a small piece of barleycorn, for she had been without a morsel to eat for two days.

"You poor little creature," said the field mouse, who was really a good old field mouse, "come into my warm room and dine with me." She was very pleased with Tiny, so she said, "You are quite welcome to stay with me all the winter, if you like, but you must keep my rooms clean and neat, and tell me stories, for I should like to hear them very much." And Tiny did all the field mouse asked her, and found herself very comfortable.

*"You poor little creature," said the field mouse.*

"We shall have a visitor soon," said the field mouse one day. "My neighbor pays me a visit once a week. He is better off than I am; he has large rooms, and wears a beautiful black velvet coat. If you could only have him for a husband, you would be well provided for indeed. But he is blind, so you must tell him some of your prettiest stories."

But Tiny did not feel at all interested about this neighbor, for he was a mole. However, he came and paid his visit dressed in his black velvet coat.

"He is very rich and learned, and his house is twenty times larger than mine," said the field mouse.

He was rich and learned, no doubt, but he always spoke slightingly of the sun and the pretty flowers, because he had never seen them. Tiny was obliged to sing to him "Ladybird, ladybird, fly away home" and many other pretty songs. And the mole fell in love with her because she had such a sweet voice; but he said nothing yet, for he was very cautious.

A short time before, the mole had dug a long passage under the earth, which led from the dwelling of the field mouse to his own, and here she had permission to walk with Tiny whenever she liked. But he warned them not to be alarmed at the sight of a dead bird which lay in the passage. It was a perfect bird, with a beak and feathers, and could not have been dead long, and was lying just where the mole had made his passage. The mole took a piece of phosphorescent wood in his mouth, and it glittered like fire in the dark; then he went before them to light them through the long, dark passage. When they came to the spot where the dead bird lay, the mole pushed his broad nose through the ceiling, the earth gave way, so that there was a large hole, and the daylight shone into the passage. In the middle of the floor lay a dead swallow, his beautiful wings pulled close to his sides, his feet and his head drawn up under his feathers; the poor bird had evidently died of the cold.

It made little Tiny very sad to see it, for she did so love the little birds; all summer they had sung and twittered for her so beautifully. But the mole pushed it aside with his crooked legs, and said, "He will sing no more now. How miserable it must be to be born a little bird! I am thankful that none of my children will ever be birds, for they can do nothing but cry, 'Tweet, tweet,' and always die of hunger in the winter."

"Yes, you may well say that, as a clever man!" exclaimed the field mouse. "What is the use of his twittering, for when winter comes he must either starve or be frozen to death. Still birds are very high bred."

Tiny said nothing; but when the two others had turned their backs on the bird, she stooped down and stroked aside the soft feathers which covered the head, and kissed the closed eyelids. "Perhaps this was the one who sang to me so sweetly in the summer," she said; "and how much pleasure it gave me, you dear, pretty bird."

The mole now stopped up the hole through which the daylight shone, and then accompanied the lady home. But during the night Tiny could not sleep, so she got out of bed and wove a large, beautiful carpet of hay, then she carried it to the dead bird, and spread it over him with some down from the flowers which she had found in the field mouse's room. It was as soft as wool, and she spread some of it on each side of the bird, so that he might lie warmly in the cold earth. "Farewell, you pretty little bird," said she, "farewell; thank you for your delightful singing during the summer, when all the trees were green, and the warm sun shone upon us." Then she laid her head on the bird's breast, but she was alarmed immediately, for it seemed as if something inside the bird went "thump, thump." It was the bird's heart—he was not really dead, only benumbed with the cold, and the warmth had restored him to life. In autumn, all the swallows fly away into warm countries, but if one happens to linger, the cold seizes it, the swallow becomes frozen, and falls down as if dead; it remains where it fell, and the cold snow covers it.

Tiny trembled very much; she was quite frightened, for the bird was large, a great deal larger than herself—she was only an inch high. But she took courage, laid the wool more thickly over the poor swallow, and then took a leaf which she had used for her own counterpane, and laid it over the head of the poor bird. The next morning she stole out to see him again. He was alive but very weak; he could only open his eyes for a moment to look at Tiny, who stood by holding a piece of decayed wood in her hand, for she had no other lantern. "Thank you, pretty little maiden," said the sick swallow; "I have been so nicely warmed, that I shall soon regain my strength, and be able to fly about again in the warm sunshine."

"Oh," said she, "it is cold out of doors now; it snows and freezes. Stay in your warm bed; I will take care of you."

Then she brought the swallow some water in a flower leaf, and after he had drank, he told her that he had wounded one of his wings in a thornbush, and could not fly as fast as the others, who were now far away on their journey to warm countries. Then at last he had fallen to the earth, and could remember no more, nor how he came to be where she had found him. The whole winter the swallow remained underground, and Tiny nursed him with care and love. Neither the mole nor the field mouse knew anything about it, for they did not like swallows. Very soon the springtime came, and the sun warmed the earth. Then the swallow bade farewell to Tiny, and she opened the hole in the ceiling which the mole had made. The sun shone in upon them so beautifully that the swallow asked her if she would go with him; she could sit on his back, he said, and he would fly away with her into the green woods. But Tiny knew it would make the field mouse very grieved if she left her in that manner, so she said, "No, I cannot."

"Farewell, then, farewell, you good, pretty little maiden," said the swallow; and he flew out into the sunshine.

Tiny looked after him, and tears rose in her eyes. She was very fond of the poor swallow.

"Tweet, tweet," sang the bird, as he flew out into the green woods, and Tiny felt very sad. She was not allowed to go out into the warm sunshine. The corn which had been sown in the field over the house of the field mouse had grown up high into the air, and formed a thick wood to Tiny, who was only an inch in height.

"You are going to be married, Tiny," said the field mouse. "My neighbor has asked for you. What good fortune for a poor child like you. Now we will prepare your wedding clothes. They must be both woolen and linen. Nothing must be wanting when you are the mole's wife."

Tiny had to turn the spindle, and the field mouse hired four spiders, who were to weave day and night. Every evening the mole visited her, and was continually speaking of the time when the summer would be over. Then he would keep his wedding day with Tiny; but now the heat of the sun was so great that it burned the earth, and made it quite hard, like a stone. As soon as the summer was over, the wedding should take place. But Tiny was not at all pleased, for she did not like the tiresome mole. Every morning when the sun rose, and every evening when it went down, she would creep out of the door, and as the wind blew aside the ears of corn so that she could see the blue sky, she thought how beautiful and bright it seemed out there, and wished so much to see her dear swallow again. But he never returned, for by this time he had flown far away into the lovely green forest.

When autumn arrived, Tiny had her outfit quite ready; and the field mouse said to her, "In four weeks the wedding must take place."

Then Tiny wept, and said she would not marry the disagreeable mole.

"Nonsense," replied the field mouse. "Now don't be obstinate, or I shall bite you with my white teeth. He is a very handsome mole;

the queen herself does not wear more beautiful velvets and furs. His kitchen and cellars are quite full. You ought to be very thankful for such good fortune."

So the wedding day was fixed, on which the mole was to fetch Tiny away to live with him, deep under the earth, and never again to see the warm sun, because he did not like it. The poor child was very unhappy at the thought of saying farewell to the beautiful sun, and as the field mouse had given her permission to stand at the door, she went to look at it once more.

"Farewell, bright sun," she cried, stretching out her arm towards it, and then she walked a short distance from the house, for the corn had been cut, and only the dry stubble remained in the fields. "Farewell, farewell," she repeated, twining her arm around a little red flower that grew just by her side. "Greet the little swallow from me, if you should see him again."

"Tweet, tweet," sounded over her head suddenly. She looked up, and there was the swallow himself flying close by! As soon as he spied Tiny, he was delighted, and then she told him how unwilling she felt to marry the ugly mole, and to live always beneath the earth, and never to see the bright sun any more, and as she told him she wept.

"Cold winter is coming," said the swallow, "and I am going to fly away into warmer countries. Will you go with me? You can sit on my back, and fasten yourself on with your sash. Then we can fly away from the ugly mole and his gloomy rooms—far away, over the mountains, into warmer countries, where the sun shines more brightly than here; where it is always summer, and the flowers bloom in greater beauty. Fly now with me, dear little Tiny; you saved my life when I lay frozen in that dark passage."

"Yes, I will go with you," said Tiny; and she seated herself on the bird's back, with her feet on his outstretched wings, and tied her girdle to one of his strongest feathers.

Then the swallow rose in the air, and flew over forest and over sea, high above the highest mountains, covered with eternal snow. Tiny would have been frozen in the cold air, but she crept under the bird's warm feathers, keeping her little head uncovered, so that she might admire the beautiful lands over which they passed. At last they reached the warm countries, where the sun shines brightly, and the sky seems so much higher above the earth. Here, on the hedges, and by the wayside, grew purple, green, and white grapes; lemons and oranges hung from trees in the woods, and the air was fragrant with myrtles and orange blossoms. Beautiful children ran along the country lanes, playing with large gay butterflies, and as the swallow flew farther and farther, every place appeared still more lovely.

At last they came to a blue lake, and by the side of it, shaded by trees of the deepest green, stood a palace of dazzling white marble, built in the olden times. Vines clustered around its lofty pillars, and at the top were many swallows' nests, and one of these was the home of the swallow who carried Tiny.

"This is my house," said the swallow; "but it would not do for you to live there—you would not be comfortable. You must choose for yourself one of those lovely flowers, and I will put you down upon it, and then you shall have everything that you can wish to make you happy."

"That will be delightful," she said, and clapped her little hands for joy.

A large marble pillar lay on the ground, which, in falling, had been broken into three pieces. Between these pieces grew the most beautiful large white flowers, so the swallow flew down with Tiny, and placed her on one of the broad leaves. But how surprised she was to see in the middle of the flower, a tiny little man, as white and transparent as if he had been made of crystal! He had a gold crown on his head, and delicate wings at his shoulders, and was not much larger than Tiny herself. He was the angel of the flower; for a tiny man and a tiny woman dwell in every flower; and this was the king of them all.

"Oh, how beautiful he is!" whispered Tiny to the swallow.

The little prince was at first quite frightened at the bird, who was like a giant, compared to such a delicate little creature as himself, but

*At last they reached the warm countries, where the sun shines brightly.*

when he saw Tiny, he was delighted, and thought her the prettiest little maiden he had ever seen. He took the gold crown from his head and placed it on hers, and asked her name, and if she would be his wife, and queen over all the flowers.

This certainly was a very different sort of husband to the son of a toad, or the mole, with his black velvet and fur, so she said "Yes" to the handsome prince. Then all the flowers opened, and out of each came a little lady or a tiny lord, all so pretty it was quite a pleasure to look at them. Each of them brought Tiny a present; but the best gift was a pair of beautiful wings, which had belonged to a large white fly, and which they fastened to Tiny's shoulders, so that she might fly from flower to flower. Then there was much rejoicing, and the little swallow who sat above them in his nest was asked to sing a wedding song, which he did as well as he could; but in his heart he felt sad, for he was very fond of Tiny, and would have liked never to part from her again.

"You must not be called Tiny any more," said the spirit of the flowers to her. "It is an ugly name, and you are so very pretty. We will call you Maia."

"Farewell, farewell," said the swallow, with a heavy heart as he left the warm countries to fly back into Denmark. There he had a nest over the window of a house in which dwelt the writer of fairy tales. The swallow sang, "Tweet, tweet," and from his song came the whole story.

*She said "Yes" to the handsome prince.*

23

# THE EMPEROR'S NEW CLOTHES

Many, many years ago lived an emperor, who thought so much of new clothes that he spent all his money in order to obtain them: his only ambition was to be always well dressed. He did not care for his soldiers, and the theater did not amuse him; the only thing, in fact, he thought anything of was to drive out and show off a new suit of clothes. He had a coat for every hour of the day; and as one would say of a king, "He is in his cabinet," so one could say of him, "The emperor is in his dressing room."

The great city where he resided was very gay; every day many strangers from all parts of the globe arrived. One day two swindlers came to this city. They made people believe that they were weavers, and declared they could manufacture the finest cloth to be imagined. Their colors and patterns, they said, were not only exceptionally beautiful, but the clothes made of their material possessed the wonderful quality of being invisible to any man who was unfit for his office or unpardonably stupid.

"That must be wonderful cloth," thought the emperor. "If I were to be dressed in a suit made of this cloth I should be able to find out which men in my empire are unfit for their places, and I could distinguish the clever from the stupid. I must have this cloth woven for me without delay." And he gave a large sum of money to the swindlers, in advance, that they should set to work without any loss of time. They set up two looms, and pretended to be very hard at work, but they did nothing whatsoever on the looms. They asked for the finest silk and the most precious gold cloth—all they got they did away with, and worked at the empty looms till late at night.

"I should very much like to know how they are getting on with the cloth," thought the emperor. But he felt rather uneasy when he remembered that whoever who was not fit for his office could not see it. Personally, he was of the opinion that he had nothing to fear, yet he thought it advisable to send somebody else first to see how matters stood. Everybody in the town knew what a remarkable quality the stuff possessed, and all were anxious to see how bad or stupid their neighbors were.

"I shall send my honest old minister to the weavers," thought the emperor. "He can judge best how the stuff looks, for he is intelligent, and nobody understands his office better than he."

The good old minister went into the room where the swindlers sat before the empty looms. "Heaven preserve us!" he thought, and opened his eyes wide, "I cannot see anything at all," but he did not say so. Both swindlers requested him to come near, and asked him if he did not admire the exquisite pattern and the beautiful colors, pointing to the empty looms. The poor old minister tried his very best, but he could see nothing, for there was nothing to be seen. "Oh dear," he thought, "can I be so stupid? I should never have thought so, and nobody must know it! Is it possible that I am not fit for my office? No, no, I cannot say that I am unable to see the cloth."

"Now, have you got nothing to say?" said one of the swindlers, while he pretended to be busily weaving.

"Oh, it is very pretty, exceedingly beautiful," replied the old minister looking through his glasses. "What a beautiful pattern, what brilliant colors! I shall tell the emperor that I like the cloth very much."

"We are pleased to hear that," said the two weavers, and described to him the colors and explained the curious pattern. The old minister listened attentively, that he might relate to the emperor what they said, and so he did.

Now the swindlers asked for more money, silk, and gold cloth, which they required for weaving. They kept everything for themselves, and not a thread came near the loom, but they continued, as hitherto, to work at the empty looms.

Soon afterwards the emperor sent another honest courtier to the weavers to see how they were getting on, and if the cloth was nearly finished. Like the old minister, he looked and looked but could see nothing, as there was nothing to be seen.

"Is it not a beautiful piece of cloth?" asked the two swindlers, showing and explaining the magnificent pattern, which, however, did not exist.

"I am not stupid," said the man. "It is therefore my good appointment for which I am not fit. It is very strange, but I must not let anyone know it"; and he praised the cloth, which he did not see, and expressed his joy at the beautiful colors and the fine pattern. "It is very excellent," he said to the emperor.

Everybody in the whole town talked about the precious cloth. At last the emperor wished to see it himself, while it was still on the loom. With a number of courtiers, including the two who had already been there, he went to the two clever swindlers, who now worked as hard as they could, but without using any thread.

"Is it not magnificent?" said the two old statesmen who had been there before. "Your Majesty must admire the colors and the pattern." And then they pointed to the empty looms, for they imagined the others could see the cloth.

"What is this?" thought the emperor, "I do not see anything at all. That is terrible! Am I stupid? Am I unfit to be emperor? That would indeed be the most dreadful thing that could happen to me."

"Really," he said, turning to the weavers, "your cloth has our most gracious approval"; and nodding contentedly, he looked at the empty loom, for he did not like to say that he saw nothing. All his attendants, who were with him, looked and looked, and although they could not see anything more than the others, they said, like the emperor, "It is very beautiful," and all advised him to wear the new magnificent clothes at a great procession which was soon to take place. "It is magnificent, beautiful, excellent," one heard them say; everybody seemed to be delighted, and the emperor appointed the two swindlers "Imperial Court weavers."

The whole night previous to the day on which the procession was to take place, the swindlers pretended to work, and burned more than sixteen candles, so that people should see that they were busy finishing the emperor's new suit. They pretended to take the cloth from the loom, and snipped about in the air with big scissors, and sewed with needles without thread, and said at last: "The emperor's new suit is ready now."

The emperor and all his barons then came to the hall; the swindlers held their arms up as if they held something in their hands and said: "These are the trousers!" "This is the coat!" and "Here is the cloak!" and so on. "They are all as light as a cobweb, and one will feel as if one had nothing at all upon the body, but that is just the beauty of them."

"Indeed!" said all the courtiers; but they could not see anything, for there was nothing to be seen.

"Does it please Your Majesty now to graciously undress," said the swindlers, "that we may assist Your Majesty in putting on the new suit before the large looking-glass?"

The emperor undressed, and the swindlers pretended to put the new suit upon him, one piece after another; and the emperor looked at himself in the glass from every side.

"How well they look! How well they fit!" said all. "What a beautiful pattern! What fine colors! That is a magnificent suit of clothes!"

The master of the ceremonies announced that the bearers of the canopy, which was to be carried in the procession, were ready.

"I am ready," said the emperor. "Does my suit not fit me marvelously?" Then he turned once more to the looking-glass, that people should think he admired his garments.

The chamberlains, who were to carry the train, stretched their hands to the ground as if they lifted up a train, and pretended to hold something in their hands; they did not like people to know that they could not see anything.

The emperor marched in the procession under the beautiful canopy, and all who saw him in the street and out of the windows exclaimed: "Indeed, the emperor's new suit is incomparable! What a long train he has! How well it fits him!" Nobody wished to let others know he saw nothing, for then he would have been unfit for his office or too stupid. Never were emperor's clothes more admired.

"But he has nothing on at all," said a little child at last.

"Good heavens! Listen to the voice of an innocent child," said the father, and one whispered to the other what the child had said. "But he has nothing on at all," cried all the people at last. That made a deep impression upon the emperor, for it seemed to him that they were right; but he thought to himself, "Now I must bear up to the end." And the chamberlains walked with still greater dignity, as if they carried the train which did not exist.

*"But he has nothing on at all,"* said a little child at last.

*There were princesses enough, but it was difficult to find out whether they were real ones.*

# THE PRINCESS AND THE PEA

Once upon a time there was a prince who wanted to marry a princess; but she would have to be a real princess. He traveled all over the world to find one, but nowhere could he get what he wanted. There were princesses enough, but it was difficult to find out whether they were real ones. There was always something about them that was not as it should be. So he came home again and was sad, for he would have liked very much to have a real princess.

One evening a terrible storm came on; there was thunder and lightning, and the rain poured down in torrents. Suddenly a knocking was heard at the city gate, and the old king went to open it.

It was a princess standing out there in front of the gate. But—good gracious!—what a sight the rain and the wind had made her look. The water ran down from her hair and clothes; it ran down into the toes of her shoes and out again at the heels. And yet she said that she was a real princess.

"Well, we'll soon find that out," thought the old queen. But she said nothing, went into the bedroom, took all the bedding off the bedstead, and laid a pea on the bottom; then she took twenty mattresses and laid them on the pea, and then twenty feather beds on top of the mattresses.

On this the princess had to lie all night. In the morning she was asked how she had slept.

"Oh, very badly!" said she. "I have scarcely closed my eyes all night.

Heaven only knows what was in the bed, but I was lying on something hard, so that I am black and blue all over my body. It's horrible!"

Now they knew that she was a real princess because she had felt the pea right through the twenty mattresses and the twenty feather beds.

Nobody but a real princess could be as sensitive as that.

So the prince took her for his wife, for now he knew that he had a real princess; and the pea was put in the museum, where it may still be seen, if no one has stolen it.

There, that is a true story.

*It was the Snow Queen.*

# THE SNOW QUEEN

## FIRST STORY

### WHICH DESCRIBES A LOOKING-GLASS AND THE BROKEN FRAGMENTS

You must attend to the commencement of this story, for when we get to the end we shall know more than we do now about a very wicked hobgoblin; he was one of the very worst, for he was a real demon. One day, when he was in a merry mood, he made a looking-glass which had the power of making everything good or beautiful that was reflected in it almost shrink to nothing, while everything that was worthless and bad looked increased in size and worse than ever. The loveliest landscapes appeared like boiled spinach, and the people became hideous, and looked as if they stood on their heads and had no bodies. Their countenances were so distorted that no one could recognize them, and even one freckle on the face appeared to spread over the whole of the nose and mouth. The demon said this was very amusing. When a good or pious thought passed through the mind of anyone, it was misrepresented in the glass; and then how the demon laughed at his cunning invention. All who went to the demon's school—for he kept a school—talked everywhere of the wonders they had seen, and declared that people could now, for the first time, see what the world and mankind were really like. They carried the glass about everywhere, till at last there was not a land nor a people who had not been looked at through this distorted mirror. They wanted even to fly with it up to heaven to see the angels, but the higher they flew the more slippery the glass became, and they could scarcely hold it, till at last it slipped from their hands, fell to the earth, and was broken into millions of pieces.

But now the looking-glass caused more unhappiness than ever, for some of the fragments were not so large as a grain of sand, and they flew about the world into every country. When one of these tiny atoms flew into a person's eye, it stuck there unknown to him, and from that moment he saw everything through a distorted medium, or could see only the worst side of what he looked at, for even the smallest fragment retained the same power which had belonged to the whole mirror. A few persons even got a fragment of the looking-glass in their hearts, and this was very terrible, for their hearts became cold like a lump of ice. A few of the pieces were so large that they could be used as windowpanes; it would have been a sad thing to look at our friends through them. Other pieces were made into spectacles; this was dreadful for those who wore them, for they could see nothing either rightly or justly.

At all this the wicked demon laughed till his sides shook—it tickled him so to see the mischief he had done. There were still a number of these little fragments of glass floating about in the air, and now you shall hear what happened with one of them.

## Second Story

### A Little Boy and a Little Girl

In a large town, full of houses and people, there is not room for everybody to have even a little garden, therefore they are obliged to be satisfied with a few flowers in flowerpots. In one of these large towns lived two poor children who had a garden larger and better than a few flowerpots. They were not brother and sister, but they loved each other almost as much as if they had been. Their parents lived opposite to each other in two garrets, where the roofs of neighboring houses projected out towards each other and the water pipe ran between them. In each house was a little window, so that anyone could step across the gutter from one window to the other. The parents of these children each had a large wooden box in which they cultivated kitchen herbs for their own use, and a little rosebush in each box, which grew splendidly. Now after a while the parents decided to place these two boxes across the water pipe, so that they reached from one window to the other and looked like two banks of flowers. Sweet peas drooped over the boxes, and the rosebushes shot forth long branches, which were trained around the windows and clustered together almost like a triumphal arch of leaves and flowers. The boxes were very high, and the children knew they must not climb upon them without permission, but they were often, however, allowed to step out together and sit upon their little stools under the rosebushes, or play quietly.

In winter all this pleasure came to an end, for the windows were sometimes quite frozen over. But then they would warm copper pennies on the stove, and hold the warm pennies against the frozen pane; there would be very soon a little round hole through which they could peep, and the soft bright eyes of the little boy and girl would beam through the hole at each window as they looked at each other. Their names were Kay and Gerda. In summer they could be together with one jump

*They were often allowed to step out together and sit upon their little stools under the rosebushes.*

from the window, but in winter they had to go up and down the long staircase, and out through the snow before they could meet.

"See there are the white bees swarming," said Kay's old grandmother one day when it was snowing.

"Have they a queen bee?" asked the little boy, for he knew that the real bees had a queen.

"To be sure they have," said the grandmother. "She is flying there where the swarm is thickest. She is the largest of them all, and never remains on the earth, but flies up to the dark clouds. Often at midnight she flies through the streets of the town, and looks in at the windows, and then the ice freezes on the panes into wonderful shapes that look like flowers and castles."

"Yes, I have seen them," said both the children, and they knew it must be true.

"Can the Snow Queen come in here?" asked the little girl.

"Just let her come," said the boy, "I'll set her on the stove and then she'll melt."

Then the grandmother smoothed his hair and told him some more tales. One evening, when little Kay was at home, half undressed, he climbed on a chair by the window and peeped out through the little hole. A few flakes of snow were falling, and one of them, rather larger than the rest, alighted on the edge of one of the flower boxes. This snowflake grew larger and larger, till at last it became the figure of a woman, dressed in garments of white gauze, which looked like millions of starry snowflakes linked together. She was fair and beautiful, but made of ice—shining and glittering ice. Still, she was alive and her eyes sparkled like bright stars, but there was neither peace nor rest in their glance. She nodded towards the window and waved her hand. The little boy was frightened and sprang from the chair; at the same moment it seemed as if a large bird flew by the window.

On the following day there was a clear frost, and very soon came the spring. The sun shone, the young green leaves burst forth, the swallows built their nests, windows were opened, and the children sat once more in the garden on the roof, high above all the other rooms. How beautiful the roses blossomed this summer. The little girl had learned a hymn in which roses were spoken of, and then she thought of their own roses, and she sang the hymn to the little boy, and he sang too:

*"Roses bloom and cease to be,*
*But we shall the Christ-child see."*

Then the little ones held each other by the hand, and kissed the roses, and looked at the bright sunshine, and spoke to it as if the Christ-child were there. Those were splendid summer days. How beautiful and fresh it was out among the rosebushes, which seemed as if they would never leave off blooming. One day Kay and Gerda sat looking at a book full of pictures of animals and birds, and then just as the clock in the church tower struck twelve, Kay said, "Oh, something has struck my heart!" and soon after, "There is something in my eye."

The little girl put her arm around his neck, and looked into his eye, but she could see nothing.

"I think it is gone," he said. But it was not gone; it was one of those bits of the looking-glass—that magic mirror of which we have spoken—the ugly glass which made everything great and good appear small and ugly, while all that was wicked and bad became more visible, and every little fault could be plainly seen. Poor little Kay had also received a small grain in his heart, which very quickly turned to a lump of ice. He felt no more pain, but the glass was there still. "Why do you cry?" said he at last. "It makes you look ugly. There is nothing the matter with me now. Oh, see!" he cried suddenly. "That rose is worm-eaten, and this one is quite crooked. After all they are ugly roses, just like the box in which they stand," and then he kicked the boxes with his foot, and pulled off the two roses.

"Kay, what are you doing?" cried the little girl; and then, when he saw how frightened she was, he tore off another rose, and jumped through his own window away from little Gerda.

When she afterwards brought out the picture book, he said it was "only fit for babies in long clothes," and when grandmother told any stories, he would interrupt her with "but"; or, when he could manage it, he would get behind her chair, put on a pair of spectacles, and imitate her very cleverly, to make people laugh. By and by he began to mimic the speech and gait of persons in the street. All that was peculiar or disagreeable in a person he would imitate directly, and people said, "That boy will be very clever; he has a remarkable genius." But it was the piece of glass in his eye, and the coldness in his heart, that made him act like this. He would even tease little Gerda, who loved him with all her heart. His games, too, were quite different; they were not so childish. One winter's day, when it snowed, he brought out a burning-glass, then he held out the tail of his blue coat, and let the snowflakes fall upon it. "Look in this glass, Gerda," said he; and she saw how every flake of snow was magnified, and looked like a beautiful flower or a glittering star. "Is it not clever?" said Kay, "And much more interesting than looking at real flowers. There is not a single fault in it, and the snowflakes are quite perfect till they begin to melt."

Soon after, Kay made his appearance in large thick gloves, and with his sled at his back. He called up to Gerda, "I've got to leave to go into the great square, where the other boys play and ride." And away he went.

In the great square, the boldest among the boys would often tie their sleds to the country people's carts, and go with them a good way. This was capital. But while they were all amusing themselves, and Kay with them, a great sled came by; it was painted white, and in it sat someone wrapped in a rough white fur, and wearing a white cap. The sled drove twice around the square, and Kay fastened his own little sled to it, so that when it went away, he followed with it. It went faster and faster right through the next street, and then the person who drove turned around and nodded pleasantly to Kay, just as if they were acquainted with each other, but whenever Kay wished to loosen his little sled the driver nodded again, so Kay sat still, and they drove out through the town gate. Then the snow began to fall so heavily that the little boy could not see a hand's breadth before him, but still they drove on; then he suddenly loosened the cord so that the large sled might go on without him, but it was of no use, his little carriage held fast, and away they went like the wind. Then he called out loudly, but nobody heard him, while the snow beat upon him, and the sled flew onwards. Every now and then it gave a jump as if it were going over hedges and ditches. The boy was frightened, and tried to say a prayer, but he could remember nothing but the multiplication table.

The snowflakes became larger and larger, till they appeared like great white chickens. All at once they sprang on one side, the great sled stopped, and the person who had driven it rose up. The fur and the cap, which were made entirely of snow, fell off, and he saw a lady, tall and white—it was the Snow Queen.

"We have driven well," said she, "but why do you tremble? Here, creep into my warm fur." Then she seated him beside her in the sled, and as she wrapped the fur around him he felt as if he were sinking into a snowdrift.

"Are you still cold?" she asked, as she kissed him on the forehead. The kiss was colder than ice; it went quite through to his heart, which was already almost a lump of ice. He felt as if he were going to die, but only for a moment: he soon seemed quite well again, and did not notice the cold around him.

"My sled! Don't forget my sled," was his first thought, and then he looked and saw that it was bound fast to one of the white chickens, which flew behind him with the sled at its back. The Snow Queen kissed little Kay again, and by this time he had forgotten little Gerda, his grandmother, and all at home.

"Now you must have no more kisses," she said, "or I should kiss you to death."

Kay looked at her, and saw that she was so beautiful, he could not imagine a more lovely and intelligent face—she did not now seem to be made of ice, as when he had seen her through his window, and she had nodded to him. In his eyes she was perfect, and he did not feel at all afraid. He told her he could do mental arithmetic, as far as fractions, and that he knew the number of square miles and the number of inhabitants in the country. And she always smiled so that he thought he did not know enough yet, and she looked around the vast expanse as she flew higher and higher with him upon a black cloud, while the storm blew and howled as if it were singing old songs. They flew over woods and lakes, over sea and land; below them roared the wild wind; the wolves howled and the snow crackled; over them flew the black screaming crows, and above all shone the moon, clear and bright—and so Kay passed through the long winter's night, and by day he slept at the feet of the Snow Queen.

## THIRD STORY

### THE FLOWER GARDEN OF THE WOMAN WHO COULD CONJURE

But how fared little Gerda during Kay's absence? What had become of him, no one knew, nor could anyone give the slightest information, except for the boys, who said that he had tied his sled to another very large one, which had driven through the street, and out at the town gate. Nobody knew where it went; many tears were shed for him, and little Gerda wept bitterly for a long time. She said she knew he must be dead; that he was drowned in the river which flowed close by the school. Oh, indeed those long winter days were very dreary. But at last spring came, with warm sunshine. "Kay is dead and gone," said little Gerda.

"I don't believe it," said the sunshine.

"He is dead and gone," she said to the sparrows.

"We don't believe it," they replied; and at last little Gerda began to doubt it herself. "I will put on my new red shoes," she said one morning, "those that Kay has never seen, and then I will go down to the river, and ask for him." It was quite early when she kissed her old grandmother, who was still asleep; then she put on her red shoes, and went quite alone out of the town gates toward the river. "Is it true that you have taken my little playmate away from me?" said she to the river. "I will give you my red shoes if you will give him back to me." And it seemed as if the waves nodded to her in a strange manner.

Then she took off her red shoes, which she liked better than anything else, and threw them both into the river, but they fell near the bank, and the little waves carried them back to the land, just as if the river would not take from her what she loved best, because they could not give her back little Kay. But she thought the shoes had not been thrown out far enough. Then she crept into a boat that lay among the reeds, and threw the shoes again from the farther end of the boat into the water, but the boat was not fastened, and her movement sent it gliding away from the land. When she saw this she hastened to reach the end of the boat, but before she could do so it was more than a yard from the bank, and drifting away faster than ever. Then little Gerda was very much frightened, and began to cry, but no one heard her except the sparrows, and they could not carry her to land, though they flew along by the shore, and sang, as if to comfort her, "Here we are! Here we are!" The boat floated with the stream; little Gerda sat quite still with only her stockings on her feet; the red shoes floated after her, but she could not reach them because the boat kept so far ahead. The banks on each side of the river were very pretty. There were beautiful flowers, old trees, sloping fields in which cows and sheep were grazing, but not a man to be seen. Perhaps the river will carry me to little Kay, thought Gerda, and then she became more cheerful, and raised her head, and looked at the beautiful green banks; and so the boat sailed on for hours.

At length she came to a large cherry orchard, in which stood a small red house with strange red and blue windows. It also had a thatched roof, and outside were two wooden soldiers that presented arms to her as she sailed past. Gerda called out to them, for she thought they were alive, but of course they did not answer; and as the boat drifted nearer to the shore, she saw what they really were. Then Gerda called still louder, and there came a very old woman out of the house, leaning on a crutch. She wore a large hat to shade her from the sun, and on it were painted all sorts of pretty flowers.

"You poor little child," said the old woman, "how did you manage to come all this distance into the wide world on such a rapid rolling stream?" And then the old woman walked in the water, seized the boat with her crutch, drew it to land, and lifted Gerda out. And Gerda was glad to feel herself on dry ground, although she was rather afraid of the strange old woman. "Come and tell me who you are," said she, "and how came you here."

Then Gerda told her everything, while the old woman shook her head, and said, "Hem-hem"; and when she had finished, Gerda asked if she had not seen little Kay, and the old woman told her he had not passed by that way, but he very likely would come. So she told Gerda not to be sorrowful, but to taste the cherries and look at the flowers; they were better than any picture book, for each of them could tell a story. Then she took Gerda by the hand and led her into the little house, and the old woman closed the door. The windows were very high, and as the panes were red, blue, and yellow, the daylight shone through them in all sorts of singular colors. On the table were some beautiful cherries, and Gerda had permission to eat as many as she would. While she was eating them the old woman combed out her long flaxen ringlets with a golden comb, and the glossy curls hung down on each side of the little round pleasant face, which looked fresh and blooming as a rose.

"I have long been wishing for a dear little maiden like you," said the old woman, "and now you must stay with me, and see how happily we shall live together." And while she went on combing little Gerda's hair, the little girl thought less and less about her adopted brother Kay, for the old woman could conjure, although she was not a wicked witch; she conjured only a little for her own amusement, and now, because she wanted to keep Gerda. Therefore she went into the garden, and stretched out her crutch towards all the rose trees, beautiful though they were, and they immediately sunk into the dark earth, so that no one could tell where they had once stood. The old woman was afraid that if little Gerda saw roses she would think of those at home, and then remember little Kay, and run away.

Then she took Gerda into the flower garden. How fragrant and beautiful it was! Every flower that could be thought of for every season of the year was here in full bloom; no picture book could have more beautiful colors. Gerda jumped for joy, and played till the sun went down behind the tall cherry trees; then she slept in an elegant bed with red silk pillows, embroidered with colored violets; and then she dreamed as pleasantly as a queen on her wedding day.

The next day, and for many days after, Gerda played with the flowers in the warm sunshine. She knew every flower, and yet, although there were so many of them, it seemed as if one were missing, but which it was she could not tell. One day, however, as she sat looking at the old woman's hat with the painted flowers on it, she saw that the prettiest of them all was a rose. The old woman had forgotten to take it from her hat when she made all the roses sink into the earth. But it is difficult to keep the thoughts together in everything; one little mistake upsets all our arrangements.

"What, are there no roses here?" cried Gerda; and she ran out into the garden, and examined all the beds, and searched and searched. There was not one to be found. Then she sat down and wept, and her tears fell just on the place where one of the rose trees had sunk down. The warm tears moistened the earth, and the rose tree sprouted up at once, as blooming as when it had sunk; and Gerda embraced it and kissed the roses, and thought of the beautiful roses at home, and, with them, of little Kay.

"Oh, how I have been detained!" said the little maiden, "I wanted to seek for little Kay. Do you know where he is?" she asked the roses. "Do you think he is dead?"

And the roses answered, "No, he is not dead. We have been in the ground where all the dead lie; but Kay is not there."

"Thank you," said little Gerda, and then she went to the other flowers, and looked into their little cups, and asked, "Do you know where little Kay is?" But each flower, as it stood in the sunshine, dreamed only of its own little fairy tale of history. Not one knew anything of Kay. Gerda heard many stories from the flowers, as she asked them one after another about him.

And what said the tiger lily?

"Hark, do you hear the drum? 'Turn, turn'—there are only two notes, always 'turn, turn.' Listen to the women's song of mourning! Hear the cry of the priest! In her long red robe stands the Hindu widow by the funeral pile. The flames rise around her as she places herself on the dead body of her husband; but the Hindu woman is thinking of the living one in that circle; of him, her son, who lighted those flames. Those shining eyes trouble her heart more painfully than the flames which will soon consume her body to ashes. Can the fire of the heart be extinguished in the flames of the funeral pile?"

"I don't understand that at all," said little Gerda.

"That is my story," said the tiger lily.

What said the convolvulus?

"Near yonder narrow road stands an old knight's castle; thick ivy creeps over the old ruined walls, leaf over leaf, even to the balcony, in which stands a beautiful maiden. She bends over the balustrades, and looks up the road. No rose on its stem is fresher than she; no apple blossom, wafted by the wind, floats more lightly than she moves. Her rich silk rustles as she bends over and exclaims, 'Will he not come?'"

"Is it Kay you mean?" asked Gerda.

"I am only speaking of a story of my dream," replied the flower.

What said the little snowdrop?

"Between two trees a rope is hanging; there is a piece of board upon it; it is a swing. Two pretty little girls, in dresses white as snow, and with long green ribbons fluttering from their hats, are sitting upon it swinging. Their brother, who is taller than they are, stands in the swing; he has one arm around the rope, to steady himself; in one hand he holds a little bowl, and in the other a clay pipe; he is blowing

*Their brother stands in the swing . . . blowing bubbles.*

bubbles. As the swing goes on, the bubbles fly upward, reflecting the most beautiful varying colors. The last still hangs from the bowl of the pipe, and sways in the wind. On goes the swing; and then a little black dog comes running up. He is almost as light as the bubble, and he raises himself on his hind legs, and wants to be taken into the swing; but it does not stop, and the dog falls; then he barks and gets angry. The children stoop towards him, and the bubble bursts. A swinging plank, a light sparkling foam picture—that is my story."

"It may be all very pretty what you are telling me," said little Gerda, "but you speak so mournfully, and you do not mention little Kay at all."

What do the hyacinths say?

"There were three beautiful sisters, fair and delicate. The dress of one was red, of the second blue, and of the third pure white. Hand in hand they danced in the bright moonlight, by the calm lake; but they were human beings, not fairy elves. The sweet fragrance attracted them, and they disappeared in the wood; here the fragrance became stronger. Three coffins, in which lay the three beautiful maidens, glided from the thickest part of the forest across the lake. The fireflies flew lightly over them, like little floating torches. Do the dancing maidens sleep, or are they dead? The scent of the flower says that they are corpses. The evening bell tolls their knell."

"You make me quite sorrowful," said little Gerda; "your perfume is so strong, you make me think of the dead maidens. Ah! Is little Kay really dead then? The roses have been in the earth, and they say no."

"Cling, clang," tolled the hyacinth bells. "We are not tolling for little Kay; we do not know him. We sing our song, the only one we know."

Then Gerda went to the buttercups that were glittering among the bright green leaves.

"You are little bright suns," said Gerda. "Tell me if you know where I can find my playfellow."

And the buttercups sparkled gaily, and looked again at Gerda. What song could the buttercups sing? It was not about Kay.

"The bright warm sun shone on a little court, on the first warm day of spring. His bright beams rested on the white walls of the neighboring house; and close by bloomed the first yellow flower of the season, glittering like gold in the sun's warm ray. An old woman sat in her armchair at the house door, and her granddaughter, a poor and pretty servant maid, came to see her for a short visit. When she kissed her grandmother there was gold everywhere: the gold of the heart in that holy kiss; it was a golden morning; there was gold in the beaming sunlight, gold in the leaves of the lowly flower, and on the lips of the maiden. There, that is my story," said the buttercup.

"My poor old grandmother!" sighed Gerda. "She is longing to see me, and grieving for me as she did for little Kay; but I shall soon go home now, and take little Kay with me. It is no use asking the flowers; they know only their own songs, and can give me no information."

And then she tucked up her little dress, that she might run faster, but the narcissus caught her by the leg as she was jumping over it; so she stopped and looked at the tall yellow flower, and said, "Perhaps you may know something."

Then she stooped down quite close to the flower, and listened; and what did he say?

"I can see myself, I can see myself," said the narcissus. "Oh, how sweet is my perfume! Up in a little room with a bow window stands a little dancing girl, half undressed; she stands sometimes on one leg, and sometimes on both, and looks as if she would tread the whole world under her feet. She is nothing but an illusion. She is pouring water out of a teapot on a piece of stuff which she holds in her hand; it is her bodice. 'Cleanliness is a good thing,' she says. Her white dress hangs on a peg; it has also been washed in the teapot, and dried on the roof. She puts it on, and ties a saffron-colored handkerchief around her neck, which makes the dress look whiter. See how she stretches out her legs, as if she were showing off on a stem. I can see myself, I can see myself."

"What do I care for all that," said Gerda, "you need not tell me such stuff!" and she ran to the other end of the garden. The door was fastened, but she pressed against the rusty latch, and it gave way. The door sprang open, and little Gerda ran out with bare feet into the wide world. She looked back three times, but no one seemed to be following her. At last she could run no longer, so she sat down to rest on a great stone, and when she looked around she saw that the summer was over, and autumn very far advanced. She had known nothing of this in the beautiful garden, where the sun shone and the flowers grew all the year-round.

"Oh, how I have wasted my time!" said little Gerda. "It is autumn. I must not rest any longer," and she rose up to go on. But her little feet were wounded and sore, and everything around her looked so cold and bleak. The long willow leaves were quite yellow. The dewdrops fell like water, leaf after leaf dropped from the trees, the sloe thorn alone still bore fruit, but the sloes were sour, and set the teeth on edge. Oh, how dark and weary the whole world appeared!

## Fourth Story

### The Prince and Princess

Gerda was obliged to rest again, and just opposite the place where she sat, she saw a great crow come hopping across the snow toward her. He stood looking at her for some time, and then he wagged his head and said, "Caw, caw; good day, good day." He pronounced the words as plainly as he could, because he meant to be kind to the little girl; and then he asked her where she was going all alone in the wide world.

The word alone Gerda understood very well, and knew how much it expressed. So then she told the crow the whole story of her life and adventures, and asked him if he had seen little Kay.

The crow nodded his head very gravely, and said, "Perhaps I have— it may be."

"No! Do you think you have?" cried little Gerda, and she kissed the crow, and hugged him almost to death with joy.

"Gently, gently," said the crow. "I believe I know. I think it may be little Kay; but he has certainly forgotten you by this time for the princess."

"Does he live with a princess?" asked Gerda.

"Yes, listen," replied the crow, "but it is so difficult to speak your language. If you understand the crows' language, then I can explain it better. Do you?"

"No, I have never learned it," said Gerda, "but my grandmother understands it, and used to speak it to me. I wish I had learned it."

"It does not matter," answered the crow; "I will explain as well as I can, although it will be very badly done"; and he told her what he had heard. "In this kingdom where we now are," said he, "there lives a princess, who is so wonderfully clever that she has read all the newspapers in the world, and forgotten them too, although she is so clever. A short time ago, as she was sitting on her throne, which people say is not such an agreeable seat as is often supposed, she began to sing a song which commences in these words: 'Why should I not be married?' 'Why not indeed?' said she, and so she determined to marry if she could find a husband who knew what to say when he was spoken to, and not one who could only look grand, for that was so tiresome. Then she assembled all her court ladies together at the beat of the drum, and when they heard of her intentions they were very much pleased. 'We are so glad to hear it,' said they, 'we were talking about it ourselves the other day.' You may believe that every word I tell you is true," said the crow, "for I have a tame sweetheart who goes freely about the palace, and she told me all this."

Of course his sweetheart was a crow, for "birds of a feather flock together," and one crow always chooses another crow.

"Newspapers were published immediately, with a border of hearts, and the initials of the princess among them. They gave notice that every young man who was handsome was free to visit the castle and speak with the princess; and those who could reply loud enough to be heard when spoken to, were to make themselves quite at home at the palace; but the one who spoke best would be chosen as a husband for the princess. Yes, yes, you may believe me, it is all as true as I sit here," said the crow. "The people came in crowds. There was a great deal of crushing and running about, but no one succeeded either on the first or second day. They could all speak very well while they were outside in the streets, but when they entered the palace gates, and saw the guards in silver uniforms, and the footmen in their golden livery on the staircase, and the great halls lit up, they became quite confused. And when they stood before the throne on which the princess sat, they could do nothing but repeat the last words she had said; and she had no particular wish to hear her own words over again. It was just as if they had all taken something to make them sleepy while they were in the palace, for they did not recover themselves nor speak till they got back again into the street. There was quite a long line of them reaching from the town gate to the palace. I went myself to see them," said the crow. "They were hungry and thirsty, for at the palace they did not get even a glass of water. Some of the wisest had taken a few slices of bread and butter with them, but they did not share it with their neighbors; they thought if they went in to the princess looking hungry, there would be a better chance for themselves."

"But Kay! Tell me about little Kay!" said Gerda. "Was he among the crowd?"

"Wait a bit, we are just coming to him. It was on the third day, when there came marching cheerfully along to the palace a little personage, without horses or carriage, his eyes sparkling like yours. He had beautiful long hair, but his clothes were very poor."

"That was Kay!" said Gerda joyfully. "Oh, then I have found him"; and she clapped her hands.

"He had a little knapsack on his back," added the crow.

"No, it must have been his sled," said Gerda; "for he went away with it."

"It may have been so," said the crow; "I did not look at it very closely.

But I know from my tame sweetheart that he passed through the palace gates, saw the guards in their silver uniform, and the servants in their liveries of gold on the stairs, but he was not in the least embarrassed. 'It must be very tiresome to stand on the stairs,' he said. 'I prefer to go in.' The rooms were blazing with light. Councillors and ambassadors walked about with bare feet, carrying golden vessels; it was enough to make anyone feel serious. His boots creaked loudly as he walked, and yet he was not at all uneasy."

"It must be Kay," said Gerda, "I know he had new boots on, I have heard them creak in grandmother's room."

"They really did creak," said the crow, "yet he went boldly up to the princess herself, who was sitting on a pearl as large as a spinning wheel, and all the ladies of the court were present with their maids, and all the cavaliers with their servants; and each of the maids had another maid to wait upon her, and the cavaliers' servants had their own servants, as well as a page each. They all stood in circles around the princess, and the nearer they stood to the door, the prouder they looked. The servants' pages, who always wore slippers, could hardly be looked at, they held themselves up so proudly by the door."

"It must be quite awful," said little Gerda, "but did Kay win the princess?"

"If I had not been a crow," said he, "I would have married her myself, although I am engaged. He spoke just as well as I do, when I speak the crows' language, so I heard from my tame sweetheart. He was quite free and agreeable and said he had not come to woo the princess, but to hear her wisdom; and he was as pleased with her as she was with him."

"Oh, certainly that was Kay," said Gerda, "he was so clever; he could work mental arithmetic and fractions. Oh, will you take me to the palace?"

"It is very easy to ask that," replied the crow, "but how are we to manage it? However, I will speak about it to my tame sweetheart, and ask her advice; for I must tell you it will be very difficult to gain permission for a little girl like you to enter the palace."

"Oh, yes; but I shall gain permission easily," said Gerda, "for when Kay hears that I am here, he will come out and fetch me in immediately."

"Wait for me here by the palings," said the crow, wagging his head as he flew away.

It was late in the evening before the crow returned. "Caw, caw," he said, "she sends you greeting, and here is a little roll which she took from the kitchen for you; there is plenty of bread there, and she thinks you must be hungry. It is not possible for you to enter the palace by the front entrance. The guards in silver uniform and the servants in gold livery would not allow it. But do not cry, we will manage to get you in; my sweetheart knows a little back staircase that leads to the sleeping apartments, and she knows where to find the key."

Then they went into the garden through the great avenue, where the leaves were falling one after another, and they could see the light in the palace being put out in the same manner. And the crow led little Gerda to the back door, which stood ajar. Oh! How little Gerda's heart beat with anxiety and longing; it was just as if she were going to do something wrong, and yet she only wanted to know where little Kay was. "It must be he," she thought, "with those clear eyes, and that long hair." She could fancy she saw him smiling at her, as he used to at home, when they sat among the roses. He would certainly be glad to see her, and to hear what a long distance she had come for his sake, and to know how sorry they had been at home because he did not come back. Oh what joy and yet fear she felt! They were now on the stairs, and in a small closet at the top a lamp was burning. In the middle of the floor stood the tame crow, turning her head from side to side, and gazing at Gerda, who curtseyed as her grandmother had taught her to do.

"My betrothed has spoken so very highly of you, my little lady," said the tame crow, "your life history, Vita, as it may be called, is very touching. If you will take the lamp I will walk before you. We will go straight along this way, then we shall meet no one."

"It seems to me as if somebody were behind us," said Gerda, as something rushed by her like a shadow on the wall, and then horses with flying manes and thin legs, hunters, ladies and gentlemen on horseback, glided by her, like shadows on the wall.

"They are only dreams," said the crow, "they are coming to fetch the thoughts of the great people out hunting."

"All the better, for we shall be able to look at them in their beds more safely. I hope that when you rise to honor and favor, you will show a grateful heart."

"You may be quite sure of that," said the crow from the forest.

They now came into the first hall, the walls of which were hung with rose-colored satin, embroidered with artificial flowers. Here the dreams again flitted by them but so quickly that Gerda could not distinguish the royal persons. Each hall appeared more splendid than the last: it was enough to bewilder anyone. At length they reached a bedroom. The ceiling was like a great palm tree, with glass leaves of the most costly crystal, and over the center of the floor two beds, each resembling a lily, hung from a stem of gold. One, in which the princess lay, was white, and the other was red; and in this Gerda had to seek for little Kay. She pushed one of the red leaves aside, and saw a little brown neck. Oh, that must be Kay! She called his name out quite loud, and held the lamp over him. The dreams rushed back into the room on horseback. He woke, and turned his head around—it was not little Kay! The prince was only like him in the neck, yet still he was young and pretty. Then the princess peeped out of her white lily bed, and asked what was the matter. Then little Gerda wept and told her story, and all that the crows had done to help her.

"You poor child," said the prince and princess; then they praised the crows, and said they were not angry for what they had done, but that it must not happen again, and this time they should be rewarded.

"Would you like to have your freedom?" asked the princess. "Or would you prefer to be raised to the position of court crows, with all that is left in the kitchen for yourselves?"

Then both the crows bowed, and begged to have a fixed appointment, for they thought of their old age, and said it would be so comfortable to feel that they had provision for their old days, as they called it. And then the prince got out of his bed, and gave it up to Gerda—he could do no more; and she lay down. She folded her little hands and thought, "How good everyone is to me, men and animals too"; then she closed her eyes and fell into a sweet sleep. All the dreams came flying back again to her, and they looked like angels, and one of them drew a little sled, on which sat Kay, and he nodded to her. But all this was only a dream, and vanished as soon as she awoke.

The following day she was dressed from head to foot in silk and velvet, and they invited her to stay at the palace for a few days, and enjoy herself, but she only begged for a pair of boots, and a little carriage, and a horse to draw it, so that she might go into the wide world to seek for Kay. And she obtained not only boots, but also a muff, and she was neatly dressed; and when she was ready to go, there, at the door, she found a coach made of pure gold, with the coat-of-arms of the prince and princess shining upon it like a star, and the coachman, footman, and outriders all wearing golden crowns on their heads. The prince and princess themselves helped her into the coach, and wished her success. The forest crow, who was now married, accompanied her for the first three miles; he sat by Gerda's side, as he could not bear riding backwards. The tame crow stood in the doorway flapping her wings. She could not go with them, because she had been suffering from a headache ever since the new appointment, no doubt from eating too much. The coach was well stored with sweet cakes, and under the seat were fruit and gingerbread nuts.

"Farewell, farewell," cried the prince and princess, and little Gerda wept, and the crow wept; and then, after a few miles, the crow also said "Farewell," and this was the saddest parting. However, he flew to a tree, and stood flapping his black wings as long as he could see the coach, which glittered in the bright sunshine.

## FIFTH STORY

### LITTLE ROBBER-GIRL

The coach drove on through a thick forest, where it lighted up the way like a torch, and dazzled the eyes of some robbers, who could not bear to let it pass them unmolested.

"It is gold! It is gold!" cried they, rushing forward and seizing the horses. Then they struck the little jockeys, the coachman, and the footman dead, and pulled little Gerda out of the carriage.

"She is fat and pretty, and she has been fed with the kernels of nuts," said the old robber-woman, who had a long beard and eyebrows that hung over her eyes. "She is as good as a little lamb; how nice she will taste!" And as she said this she drew forth a shining knife that glittered horribly. "Oh!" screamed the old woman at the same moment; for her own daughter, who was holding her back, had bitten her in the ear. She was a wild and naughty girl, and the mother called her an ugly thing, and had not time to kill Gerda.

"She shall play with me," said the little robber-girl; "she shall give me her muff and her pretty dress, and sleep with me in my bed." And then she bit her mother again, and made her spring in the air, and jump about; and all the robbers laughed, and said, "See how she is dancing with her young cub."

"I will have a ride in the coach," said the little robber-girl; and she would have her own way, for she was so self-willed and obstinate.

She and Gerda seated themselves in the coach, and drove away, over stumps and stones, into the depths of the forest. The little robber-girl was about the same size as Gerda, but stronger; she had broader shoulders and a darker skin; her eyes were quite black, and she had a mournful look. She clasped little Gerda around the waist, and said:

"They shall not kill you as long as you don't make us vexed with you. I suppose you are a princess."

"No," said Gerda; and then she told her all her history, and how fond she was of little Kay.

The robber-girl looked earnestly at her, nodded her head slightly, and said, "They shan't kill you, even if I do get angry with you; for I will do it myself." And then she wiped Gerda's eyes, and stuck her own hands in the beautiful muff which was so soft and warm.

The coach stopped in the courtyard of a robber's castle, the walls of which were cracked from top to bottom. Ravens and crows flew in and out of the holes and crevices, while great bulldogs, looking as if they could swallow a man, were jumping about; but they were not allowed to bark. In the large and smoky hall, a bright fire was burning on the stone floor. There was no chimney, so the smoke went up to the ceiling, and found a way out for itself. Soup was boiling in a large cauldron, and hares and rabbits were roasting on the spit.

"You shall sleep with me and all my little animals tonight," said the robber-girl, after they had had something to eat and drink. So she took Gerda to a corner of the hall, where some straw and carpets were laid down. Above them, on laths and perches, were more than a hundred pigeons, who all seemed to be asleep, although they moved slightly when the two little girls came near them.

"These all belong to me," said the robber-girl; and she seized the nearest to her, held it by the feet, and shook it till it flapped its wings. "Kiss it," cried she, flapping it in Gerda's face. "There sit the wood pigeons," continued she, pointing to a number of laths and a cage which had been fixed into the walls, near one of the openings. "Both rascals would fly away directly if they were not closely locked up. And here is my old sweetheart, Ba"; and she dragged out a reindeer by the horn; he wore a bright copper ring around his neck, and was tied up. "We are obliged to hold him tight too, or else he would run away from us as well. I tickle his neck every evening with my sharp knife, which frightens him very much." And then the robber-girl drew a long knife from a chink in the wall, and let it slide gently over the reindeer's neck. The poor animal began to kick, and the little robber-girl laughed, and pulled down Gerda into bed with her.

"Will you have that knife with you while you are asleep?" asked Gerda, looking at it in great fright.

"I always sleep with the knife by me," said the robber-girl. "No one knows what may happen. But now tell me again all about little Kay, and why you went out into the world."

Then Gerda repeated her story over again, while the wood pigeons in the cage over her cooed, and the other pigeons slept. The little robber-girl put one arm across Gerda's neck, and held the knife in the

*"You shall sleep with me and all my little animals tonight," said the robber-girl.*

other, and was soon fast asleep and snoring. But Gerda could not close her eyes at all; she knew not whether she was to live or die. The robbers sat around the fire, singing and drinking, and the old woman stumbled about. It was a terrible sight for a little girl to witness.

Then the wood pigeons said, "Coo, coo; we have seen little Kay. A white fowl carried his sled, and he sat in the carriage of the Snow Queen, which drove through the wood while we were lying in our nest. She blew upon us, and all the young ones died excepting us two. Coo, coo."

"What are you saying up there?" cried Gerda. "Where was the Snow Queen going? Do you know anything about it?"

"She was most likely traveling to Lapland, where there is always snow and ice. Ask the reindeer that is fastened up there with a rope."

"Yes, there is always snow and ice," said the reindeer; "and it is a glorious place; you can leap and run about freely on the sparkling ice plains. The Snow Queen has her summer tent there, but her strong castle is at the North Pole, on an island called Spitzbergen."

"Oh, Kay, little Kay!" sighed Gerda.

"Lie still," said the robber-girl, "or I shall run my knife into your body."

In the morning Gerda told her all that the wood pigeons had said; and the little robber-girl looked quite serious, and nodded her head, and said, "That is all talk, that is all talk. Do you know where Lapland is?" she asked the reindeer.

"Who should know better than I do?" said the animal, while his eyes sparkled. "I was born and brought up there, and used to run about the snow-covered plains."

"Now listen," said the robber-girl; "all our men are gone away—only mother is here, and here she will stay; but at noon she always drinks out of a great bottle, and afterwards sleeps for a little while; and then, I'll do something for you." Then she jumped out of bed, clasped her mother around the neck, and pulled her by the beard, crying, "My own little nanny goat, good morning." Then her mother filliped her nose till it was quite red; yet she did it all for love.

When the mother had drunk out of the bottle, and was gone to sleep, the little robber-maiden went to the reindeer, and said, "I should like very much to tickle your neck a few times more with my knife, for it makes you look so funny; but never mind—I will untie your cord, and set you free, so that you may run away to Lapland; but you must make good use of your legs, and carry this little maiden to the castle of the Snow Queen, where her playfellow is. You have heard what she told me, for she spoke loud enough, and you were listening."

Then the reindeer jumped for joy; and the little robber-girl lifted Gerda on his back, and had the forethought to tie her on, and even to give her her own little cushion to sit on.

"Here are your fur boots for you," said she; "for it will be very cold; but I must keep the muff; it is so pretty. However, you shall not be frozen for the want of it; here are my mother's large warm mittens; they will reach up to your elbows. Let me put them on. There, now your hands look just like my mother's."

But Gerda wept for joy.

"I don't like to see you fret," said the little robber-girl; "you ought to look quite happy now; and here are two loaves and a ham, so that you need not starve." These were fastened on the reindeer, and then the little robber-maiden opened the door, coaxed in all the great dogs, and then cut the string with which the reindeer was fastened, with her sharp knife, and said, "Now run, but mind you take good care of the little girl." And then Gerda stretched out her hand, with the great mitten on it, towards the little robber-girl, and said, "Farewell," and away flew the reindeer, over stumps and stones, through the great forest, over marshes and plains, as quickly as he could. The wolves howled, and the ravens screamed; while up in the sky quivered red lights like flames of fire. "There are my old northern lights," said the reindeer; "see how they flash." And he ran on day and night still faster and faster, but the loaves and the ham were all eaten by the time they reached Lapland.

## Sixth Story

### The Lapland Woman and the Finland Woman

They stopped at a little hut; it was very mean looking; the roof sloped nearly down to the ground, and the door was so low that the family had to creep in on their hands and knees when they went in and out. There was no one at home but an old Lapland woman, who was cooking fish by the light of a train-oil lamp. The reindeer told her all about Gerda's story, after having first told his own, which seemed to him the most important, but Gerda was so pinched with the cold that she could not speak. "Oh, you poor things," said the Lapland woman, "you have a long way to go yet. You must travel more than a hundred miles farther, to Finland. The Snow Queen lives there now, and she burns Bengal lights every evening. I will write a few words on a dried stockfish, for I have no paper, and you can take it from me to the Finland woman who lives there; she can give you better information than I can."

So when Gerda was warmed, and had taken something to eat and drink, the woman wrote a few words on the dried fish, and told Gerda to take great care of it.

Then she tied her again on the reindeer, and he set off at full speed. Flash, flash, went the beautiful blue northern lights in the air the whole night long. And at length they reached Finland, and knocked at the chimney of the Finland woman's hut, for it had no door above the ground. They crept in, but it was so terribly hot inside that that woman wore scarcely any clothes; she was small and very dirty looking. She loosened little Gerda's dress, and took off the fur boots and the mittens, or Gerda would have been unable to bear the heat; and then she placed a piece of ice on the reindeer's head, and read what was written on the dried fish. After she had read it three times, she knew it by heart, so she popped the fish into the soup saucepan, as she knew it was good to eat, and she never wasted anything.

The reindeer told his own story first, and then little Gerda's, and the Finlander twinkled with her clever eyes, but she said nothing. "You are so clever," said the reindeer; "I know you can tie all the winds of the world with a piece of twine. If a sailor unties one knot, he has a fair wind; when he unties the second, it blows hard; but if the third and fourth are loosened, then comes a storm, which will root up whole forests. Cannot you give this little maiden something which will make her as strong as twelve men, to overcome the Snow Queen?"

"The power of twelve men!" said the Finland woman. "That would be of very little use." But she went to a shelf and took down and unrolled a large skin, on which were inscribed wonderful characters, and she read till the perspiration ran down from her forehead. But the reindeer begged so hard for little Gerda, and Gerda looked at the Finland woman with such beseeching tearful eyes, that her own eyes began to twinkle again; so she drew the reindeer into a corner, and whispered to him while she laid a fresh piece of ice on his head, "Little Kay is really with the Snow Queen. He finds everything there so much to his taste and his liking, that he believes it is the finest place in the world; but this is because he has a piece of broken glass in his heart, and a little piece of glass in his eye. These must be taken out, or he will never be a human being again, and the Snow Queen will retain her power over him."

"But can you not give little Gerda something to help her to conquer this power?"

"I can give her no greater power than she has already," said the woman; "don't you see how strong that is? How men and animals are obliged to serve her, and how well she has got through the world, barefooted as she is. She cannot receive any power from me greater than she now has, which consists in her own purity and innocence of heart. If she cannot herself obtain access to the Snow Queen, and remove the glass fragments from little Kay, we can do nothing to help her. Two miles from here the Snow Queen's garden begins; you can carry the little girl so far, and set her down by the large bush which stands in the snow, covered with red berries. Do not stay gossiping, but come back here as quickly as you can." Then the Finland woman lifted little Gerda upon the reindeer, and he ran away with her as quickly as he could.

"Oh, I have forgotten my boots and my mittens," cried little Gerda, as soon as she felt the cutting cold, but the reindeer dared not stop, so he ran on till he reached the bush with the red berries; here he set Gerda down, and he kissed her, and great bright tears trickled over the animal's cheeks; then he left her and ran back as fast as he could.

There stood poor Gerda, without shoes, without gloves, in the midst of cold, dreary, ice-bound Finland. She ran forward as quickly as she could, when a whole regiment of snowflakes came around her. They did not, however, fall from the sky, which was quite clear and glittering with the northern lights: the snowflakes ran along the ground, and the nearer they came to her, the larger they appeared. Gerda remembered how large and beautiful they looked through the burning-glass. But these were larger, and much more terrible, for they were alive, and were the guards of the Snow Queen, and had the strangest shapes. Some were like great porcupines, others like twisted serpents with their heads stretching out, and some few were like little fat bears with their hair bristled; but all were dazzlingly white, and all were living snowflakes.

Then little Gerda repeated the Lord's Prayer, and the cold was so great that she could see her own breath come out of her mouth like steam as she uttered the words. The steam appeared to increase as she continued her prayer, till it took the shape of little angels who grew larger the moment they touched the earth. They all wore helmets on their heads, and carried spears and shields. Their number continued to increase more and more; and by the time Gerda had finished her prayers, a whole legion stood around her. They thrust their spears into the terrible snowflakes, so that they shattered into a hundred pieces, and little Gerda could go forward with courage and safety. The angels stroked her hands and feet, so that she felt the cold less, and she hastened on to the Snow Queen's castle.

But now we must see what Kay is doing. In truth he thought not of little Gerda, and never supposed she could be standing in the front of the palace.

## SEVENTH STORY

### OF THE PALACE OF THE SNOW QUEEN AND WHAT HAPPENED THERE AT LAST

The walls of the palace were formed of drifted snow, and the windows and doors of the cutting winds. There were more than a hundred rooms in it, all as if they had been formed with snow blown together. The largest of them extended for several miles; they were all lighted up by the vivid light of the aurora, and they were so large and empty, so icy cold and glittering! There were no amusements here, not even a little bear's ball, when the storm might have been the music, and the bears could have danced on their hind legs, and shown their good manners. There were no pleasant games of snapdragon, or touch, or even a gossip over the tea table, for the young lady foxes. Empty, vast, and cold were the halls of the Snow Queen. The flickering flame of the northern lights could be plainly seen, whether they rose high or low in the heavens, from every part of the castle. In the midst of its empty, endless hall of snow was a frozen lake, broken on its surface into a thousand forms; each piece resembled another, being in itself perfect as a work of art, and in the center of this lake sat the Snow Queen, when she was at home. She called the lake "The Mirror of Reason," and said that it was the best, and indeed the only one in the world.

Little Kay was quite blue with cold, indeed almost black, but he did not feel it; for the Snow Queen had kissed away the icy shiverings, and his heart was already a lump of ice. He dragged some sharp, flat pieces of ice to and fro, and placed them together in all kinds of positions, as if he wished to make something out of them; just as we try to form various figures with little tablets of wood which we call "a Chinese puzzle." Kay's fingers were very artistic; it was the icy game of reason at which he played, and in his eyes the figures were very remarkable, and of the highest importance; this opinion was owing to the piece of glass still sticking in his eye. He composed many complete figures, forming different words, but there was one word he never could manage to form, although he wished it very much. It was the word "eternity." The Snow Queen had said to him, "When you can find out this, you shall be your own master, and I will give you the whole world and a new pair of skates." But he could not accomplish it.

"Now I must hasten away to warmer countries," said the Snow Queen. "I will go and look into the black craters of the tops of the burning mountains, Etna and Vesuvius, as they are called—I shall make them look white, which will be good for them, and for the lemons and the grapes." And away flew the Snow Queen, leaving little Kay quite alone in the great hall which was so many miles in length; so he sat and looked at his pieces of ice, and was thinking so deeply, and sat so still, that anyone might have supposed he was frozen.

Just at this moment it happened that little Gerda came through the great door of the castle. Cutting winds were raging around her, but she offered up a prayer and the winds sank down as if they were going to sleep; and she went on till she came to the large empty hall, and caught sight of Kay; she knew him directly; she flew to him and threw her arms around his neck, and held him fast, while she exclaimed, "Kay, dear little Kay, I have found you at last."

But he sat quite still, stiff and cold.

Then little Gerda wept hot tears, which fell on his breast, and penetrated into his heart, and thawed the lump of ice, and washed away the little piece of glass which had stuck there. Then he looked at her, and she sang:

*"Roses bloom and cease to be,*
*But we shall the Christ-child see."*

Then Kay burst into tears, and he wept so that the splinter of glass swam out of his eye. Then he recognized Gerda, and said, joyfully, "Gerda, dear little Gerda, where have you been all this time, and where have I been?" And he looked all around him, and said, "How cold it is, and how large and empty it all looks," and he clung to Gerda, and she laughed and wept for joy. It was so pleasing to see them that the pieces of ice even danced about; and when they were tired and went to lie down, they formed themselves into the letters of the word which the Snow Queen had said he must find out before he could be his own master, and have the whole world and a pair of new skates. Then Gerda kissed his cheeks, and they became blooming; and she kissed his eyes, and they shone like her own; she kissed his hands and his feet, and then he became quite healthy and cheerful. The Snow Queen might come home now when she pleased, for there stood his certainty of freedom, in the word she wanted, written in shining letters of ice.

Then they took each other by the hand, and went forth from the great palace of ice. They spoke of the grandmother, and of the roses on the roof, and as they went on the winds were at rest, and the sun burst forth. When they arrived at the bush with red berries, there stood the reindeer waiting for them, and he had brought another young reindeer with him, whose udders were full, and the children drank her warm milk and kissed her on the mouth. Then they carried Kay and Gerda first to the Finland woman, where they warmed themselves thoroughly in the hot room, and she gave them directions about their journey home. Next they went to the Lapland woman, who had made some new clothes for them, and put their sleighs in order. Both the reindeer ran by their side, and followed them as far as the boundaries of the country, where the first green leaves were budding. And here they took leave of the two reindeer and the Lapland woman, and all said "Farewell."

Then the birds began to twitter, and the forest too was full of green young leaves; and out of it came a beautiful horse, which Gerda remembered, for it was one which had drawn the golden coach. A young girl was riding upon it, with a shining red cap on her head, and pistols in her belt. It was the little robber-maiden, who had got tired of staying at home; she was going first to the north, and if that did not suit her, she meant to try some other part of the world. She knew Gerda directly, and Gerda remembered her: it was a joyful meeting.

"You are a fine fellow to go gadding about in this way," said she to little Kay, "I should like to know whether you deserve that anyone should go to the end of the world to find you."

But Gerda patted her cheeks, and asked after the prince and princess.

"They are gone to foreign countries," said the robber-girl.

"And the crow?" asked Gerda.

"Oh, the crow is dead," she replied; "his tame sweetheart is now a widow, and wears a bit of black worsted around her leg. She mourns very pitifully, and chatters more than ever. But now tell me how you managed to get him back."

Then Gerda and Kay told her all about it.

"Snip, snap, snare! It's all right at last," said the robber-girl.

Then she took both their hands, and promised that if ever she should pass through the town, she would call and pay them a visit. And then she rode away into the wide world. But Gerda and Kay went hand in hand towards home; and as they advanced, spring appeared more lovely with its green verdure and its beautiful flowers. Very soon they recognized the large town where they lived, and the tall steeples of the churches, in which the sweet bells were ringing a merry peal as they entered it, and found their way to their grandmother's door. They went upstairs into the little room, where all looked just as it used to do. The old clock was going "tick, tick," and the hands pointed to the time of day, but as they passed through the door into the room they perceived that they were both grown up, and had become a man and woman. The roses out on the roof were in full bloom, and peeped in at the window; and there stood the little chairs, on which they had sat when children; and Kay and Gerda seated themselves each on their own chair, and held each other by the hand, while the cold empty grandeur of the Snow Queen's palace vanished from their memories like a painful dream. The grandmother sat in God's bright sunshine, and she read aloud from the Bible, "Except ye become as little children, ye shall in no wise enter into the kingdom of God." And Kay and Gerda looked into each other's eyes, and all at once understood the words of the old song:

*"Roses bloom and cease to be,*
*But we shall the Christ-child see."*

And they both sat there, grown up, yet children at heart; and it was summer—warm, beautiful summer.

*The brave tin soldier.*

# THE BRAVE TIN SOLDIER

There were once five-and-twenty tin soldiers, who were all brothers, for they had been made out of the same old tin spoon. They shouldered arms and looked straight before them, and wore a splendid uniform, red and blue. The first thing in the world they ever heard were the words "Tin soldiers!" uttered by a little boy, who clapped his hands with delight when the lid of the box in which they lay was taken off. They were given him for a birthday present, and he stood at the table to set them up. The soldiers were all exactly alike, excepting one, who had only one leg; he had been left until last, and then there was not enough of the melted tin to finish him, so they made him to stand firmly on one leg, and this caused him to be very remarkable.

The table on which the tin soldiers stood was covered with other playthings, but the most attractive to the eye was a pretty little paper castle. Through the small windows the rooms could be seen. In front of the castle a number of little trees surrounded a piece of looking-glass, which was intended to represent a transparent lake. Swans made of wax swam on the lake, and were reflected in it. All this was very pretty, but the prettiest of all was a tiny little lady, who stood at the open door of the castle; she too was made of paper, and she wore a dress of clear muslin, with a narrow blue ribbon over her shoulders just like a scarf. In front of these was fixed a glittering tinsel rose, as large as her whole face. The little lady was a dancer, and she stretched out both her arms, and raised one of her legs so high, that the tin soldier could not see it at all, and he thought that she, like himself, had only one leg. "That is the wife for me," he thought; "but she is too grand, and lives in a castle, while I have only a box to live in, five-and-twenty of us altogether—that is no place for her. Still I must try and make her acquaintance." Then he laid himself at full length on the table behind a snuffbox that stood upon it, so that he could peep at the little delicate lady, who continued to stand on one leg without losing her balance.

When evening came, the other tin soldiers were all placed in the box, and the people of the house went to bed. Then the playthings began to have their own games together, to pay visits, to have sham fights, and to give balls. The tin soldiers rattled in their box; they wanted to get out and join the amusements, but they could not open the lid. The nutcrackers played at leapfrog, and the pencil jumped about the table. There was such a noise that the canary woke up and began to talk, and in poetry too. Only the tin soldier and the dancer remained in their places. She stood on tiptoe, with her legs stretched out, as firmly as he did on his one leg. He never took his eyes from her for even a moment. The clock struck twelve, and, with a bounce, up sprang the lid of the snuffbox; but, instead of snuff, there jumped up a little black goblin; for the snuffbox was a toy puzzle.

"Tin soldier," said the goblin, "don't wish for what does not belong to you."

But the tin soldier pretended not to hear.

"Very well; wait till tomorrow, then," said the goblin.

When the children came in the next morning, they placed the tin soldier in the window. Now, whether it was the goblin who did it, or the draft, is not known, but the window flew open, and out fell the tin soldier, heels over head, from the third story, into the street beneath. It was a terrible fall; for he came head downwards, his helmet and his bayonet stuck in between the flagstones, and his one leg up in the air. The servant maid and the little boy went downstairs straight away to look for him; but he was nowhere to be seen, although once they nearly trod upon him. If he had called out, "Here I am," it would have been all right, but he was too proud to cry out for help while he wore a uniform.

Presently it began to rain, and the drops fell faster and faster, till there was a heavy shower. When it was over, two boys happened to pass by, and one of them said, "Look, there is a tin soldier. He ought to have a boat to sail in."

So they made a boat out of a newspaper, and placed the tin soldier in it, and sent him sailing down the gutter, while the two boys ran by the side of it, and clapped their hands. Good gracious, what large waves arose in that gutter, and how fast the stream rolled on, for the rain had been very heavy. The paper boat rocked up and down, and turned itself around sometimes so quickly that the tin soldier trembled; yet he remained firm; his countenance did not change; he looked straight before him, and shouldered his musket. Suddenly the boat shot under a bridge which formed a part of a drain, and then it was as dark as the tin soldier's box.

"Where am I going now?" thought he. "This is the black goblin's fault, I am sure. Ah, well, if the little lady were only here with me in the boat, I should not care for any darkness."

Suddenly there appeared a great water rat, who lived in the drain.

"Have you a passport?" asked the rat. "Give it to me at once." But the tin soldier remained silent and held his musket tighter than ever. The boat sailed on and the rat followed it. How he did gnash his teeth and cry out to the bits of wood and straw, "Stop him, stop him; he has not paid the toll, and has not shown his pass!"

But the stream rushed on stronger and stronger. The tin soldier could already see daylight shining where the arch ended. Then he heard a roaring sound terrible enough to frighten the bravest man. At the end of the tunnel the drain fell into a large canal over a steep place, which made it as dangerous for him as a waterfall would be to us. He was too close to it to stop, so the boat rushed on, and the poor tin soldier could only hold himself as stiffly as possible, without moving an eyelid, to show that he was not afraid. The boat whirled around three or four times, and then filled with water to the very edge; nothing could save it from sinking. He now stood up to his neck in water, while deeper and deeper sank the boat, and the paper became soft and loose with the wet, till at last the water closed over the soldier's head. He thought of the elegant little dancer whom he should never see again, and the words of the song sounded in his ears:

*"Farewell, warrior! Ever brave,*
*Drifting onward to thy grave."*

Then the paper boat fell to pieces, and the soldier sank into the water and immediately afterwards was swallowed up by a great fish. Oh how dark it was inside the fish! A great deal darker than in the tunnel, and narrower too, but the tin soldier continued firm, and lay at full length shouldering his musket. The fish swam to and fro, making the most wonderful movements, but at last he became quite still. After a while, a flash of lightning seemed to pass through him, and then the daylight approached, and a voice cried out, "I declare, here is the tin soldier!"

The fish had been caught, taken to the market, and sold to the cook, who took him into the kitchen and cut him open with a large knife. She picked up the soldier and held him by the waist between her finger and thumb, and carried him into the room. They were all anxious to see this wonderful soldier who had traveled about inside a fish; but he was not at all proud. They placed him on the table, and—how many curious things do happen in the world!—there he was in the very same room from the window of which he had fallen, there were the same children, the same playthings standing on the table, and the pretty castle with the elegant little dancer at the door; she still balanced herself on one leg, and held up the other, so she was as firm as himself. It touched the tin soldier so much to see her that he almost wept tin tears, but he kept them back. He only looked at her and they both remained silent.

Presently one of the little boys took up the tin soldier, and threw him into the stove. He had no reason for doing so, therefore it must have been the fault of the black goblin who lived in the snuffbox. The flames lighted up the tin soldier as he stood, the heat was very terrible, but whether it proceeded from the real fire or from the fire of love he could not tell. Then he could see that the bright colors were faded from his uniform, but whether they had been washed off during his journey or from the effects of his sorrow, no one could say. He looked at the little lady, and she looked at him. He felt himself melting away, but he still remained firm with his gun on his shoulder.

Suddenly the door of the room flew open and the draft of air caught up the little dancer, she fluttered like a sylph right into the stove by the side of the tin soldier, and was instantly in flames and was gone. The tin soldier melted down into a lump, and the next morning, when the maid servant took the ashes out of the stove, she found him in the shape of a little tin heart. But of the little dancer nothing remained but the tinsel rose, which was burnt black as a cinder.

# THE NIGHTINGALE

In China, you know, the emperor is Chinese, and all those about him are Chinamen also. The story I am going to tell you happened a great many years ago, so it is well to hear it now before it is forgotten.

The emperor's palace was the most beautiful in the world. It was built entirely of porcelain, and very costly, but so delicate and brittle that whoever touched it was obliged to be careful. In the garden could be seen the most singular flowers, with pretty silver bells tied to them, which tinkled so that everyone who passed could not help noticing the flowers. Indeed, everything in the emperor's garden was remarkable, and it extended so far that the gardener himself did not know where it ended. Those who traveled beyond its limits knew that there was a noble forest, with lofty trees, sloping down to the deep blue sea, and the great ships sailed under the shadow of its branches. In one of these trees lived a nightingale, who sang so beautifully that even the poor fishermen, who had so many other things to do, would stop and listen. Sometimes, when they went at night to spread their nets, they would hear her sing, and say, "Oh, is not that beautiful?" But when they returned to their fishing, they forgot the bird until the next night. Then they would hear it again, and exclaim, "Oh, how beautiful is the nightingale's song!"

Travelers from every country in the world came to the city of the emperor, which they admired very much, as well as the palace and gardens; but when they heard the nightingale, they all declared it to be the best of all. And the travelers, on their return home, related what they had seen; and learned men wrote books, containing descriptions of the town, the palace, and the gardens; but they did not forget the nightingale, which was really the greatest wonder. And those who could write poetry composed beautiful verses about the nightingale, who lived in a forest near the deep sea. The books traveled all over the world, and some of them came into the hands of the emperor; and he sat in his golden chair, and, as he read, he nodded his approval every moment, for it pleased him to find such a beautiful description of his city, his palace, and his gardens. But when he came to the words "the nightingale is the most beautiful of all," he exclaimed, "What is this? I know nothing of any nightingale. Is there such a bird in my empire? And even in my garden? I have never heard of it. Something, it appears, may be learned from books."

Then he called one of his lords-in-waiting, who was so high-bred, that when any in an inferior rank to himself spoke to him, or asked him a question, he would answer, "Pooh," which means nothing.

"There is a very wonderful bird mentioned here, called a nightingale," said the emperor; "they say it is the best thing in my large kingdom. Why have I not been told of it?"

"I have never heard the name," replied the cavalier; "she has not been presented at court."

"It is my pleasure that she shall appear this evening," said the emperor; "the whole world knows what I possess better than I do myself."

"I have never heard of her," said the cavalier; "yet I will endeavor to find her."

But where was the nightingale to be found? The nobleman went upstairs and down, through halls and passages; yet none of those whom he met had heard of the bird. So he returned to the emperor, and said that it must be a fable, invented by those who had written the book. "Your imperial majesty," said he, "cannot believe everything contained in books; sometimes they are only fiction, or what is called the black art."

"But the book in which I have read this account," said the emperor, "was sent to me by the great and mighty emperor of Japan, and therefore it cannot contain a falsehood. I will hear the nightingale. She must be here this evening; she has my highest favor; and if she does not come, the whole court shall be trampled upon after supper is ended."

"Tsing-pe!" cried the lord-in-waiting, and again he ran up and downstairs, through all the halls and corridors; and half the court ran with him, for they did not like the idea of being trampled upon. There was a great inquiry about this wonderful nightingale, whom all the world knew, but who was unknown to the court.

At last they met with a poor little girl in the kitchen, who said, "Oh, yes, I know the nightingale quite well; indeed, she can sing. Every evening I have permission to take home to my poor sick mother the scraps from the table; she lives down by the seashore, and as I come back I feel tired, and I sit down in the wood to rest, and listen to the nightingale's song. Then the tears come into my eyes, and it is just as if my mother kissed me."

"Little maiden," said the lord-in-waiting, "I will obtain for you constant employment in the kitchen, and you shall have permission to see the emperor dine, if you will lead us to the nightingale; for she is invited for this evening to the palace." So she went into the wood where the nightingale sang, and half the court followed her. As they went along, a cow began lowing.

"Oh," said a young courtier, "now we have found her; what wonderful power for such a small creature; I have certainly heard it before."

"No, that is only a cow lowing," said the little girl; "we are a long way from the place yet."

Then some frogs began to croak in the marsh.

"Beautiful," said the young courtier again. "Now I hear it, tinkling like little church bells."

"No, those are frogs," said the little maiden; "but I think we shall soon hear her now," and presently the nightingale began to sing.

"Hark, hark! There she is," said the girl, "and there she sits," she added, pointing to a little gray bird who was perched on a bough.

"Is it possible?" said the lord-in-waiting, "I never imagined it would be a little, plain, simple thing like that. She has certainly changed color at seeing so many grand people around her."

"Little nightingale," cried the girl, raising her voice, "our most gracious emperor wishes you to sing before him."

"With the greatest pleasure," said the nightingale, and began to sing most delightfully.

"It sounds like tiny glass bells," said the lord-in-waiting, "and see how her little throat works. It is surprising that we have never heard this before; she will be a great success at court."

"Shall I sing once more before the emperor?" asked the nightingale, who thought he was present.

*Presently the nightingale began to sing.*

"My excellent little nightingale," said the courtier, "I have the great pleasure of inviting you to a court festival this evening, where you will gain imperial favor by your charming song."

"My song sounds best in the green wood," said the bird; but still she came willingly when she heard the emperor's wish.

The palace was elegantly decorated for the occasion. The walls and floors of porcelain glittered in the light of a thousand lamps. Beautiful flowers, around which little bells were tied, stood in the corridors: what with the running to and fro and the draft, these bells tinkled so loudly that no one could speak to be heard. In the center of the great hall, a golden perch had been fixed for the nightingale to sit on. The whole court was present, and the little kitchen maid had received permission to stand by the door. She was not installed as a real court cook. All were in full dress, and every eye was turned to the little gray bird when the emperor nodded to her to begin. The nightingale sang so sweetly that tears came into the emperor's eyes, and then rolled down his cheeks, as her song became still more touching and went to everyone's heart. The emperor was so delighted that he declared the nightingale should have his gold slipper to wear around her neck, but she declined the honor with thanks: she had been sufficiently rewarded already. "I have seen tears in an emperor's eyes," she said, "that is my richest reward. An emperor's tears have wonderful power, and are quite sufficient honor for me"; and then she sang again more enchantingly than ever.

"That singing is a lovely gift," said the ladies of the court to each other; and then they took water in their mouths to make them utter the gurgling sounds of the nightingale when they spoke to anyone, so that they might fancy themselves nightingales. And the footmen and chambermaids also expressed their satisfaction, which is saying a great deal, for they are very difficult to please. In fact, the nightingale's visit was most successful. She was now to remain at court, to have her own cage, with liberty to go out twice a day, and once during the night.

Twelve servants were appointed to attend her on these occasions, who each held her by a silken string fastened to her leg. There was certainly not much pleasure in this kind of flying.

The whole city spoke of the wonderful bird, and when two people met, one said "nightin," and the other said "gale," and they understood what was meant, for nothing else was talked of. Eleven peddlers' children were named after her, but not of them could sing a note.

One day the emperor received a large packet on which was written "The Nightingale." "Here is no doubt a new book about our celebrated bird," said the emperor.

But instead of a book, it was a work of art contained in a casket: an artificial nightingale made to look like a living one, and covered all over with diamonds, rubies, and sapphires. As soon as the artificial bird was wound up, it could sing like the real one, and could move its tail up and down, which sparkled with silver and gold. Around its neck hung a piece of ribbon, on which was written "The Emperor of Japan's nightingale is poor compared with that of the Emperor of China's."

"This is very beautiful," exclaimed all who saw it, and he who had brought the artificial bird received the title of "Imperial nightingale-bringer-in-chief."

"Now they must sing together," said the court, "and what a duet it will be." But they did not get on well, for the real nightingale sang in its own natural way, but the artificial bird sang only waltzes.

"That is not a fault," said the music master, "it is quite perfect to my taste," so then it had to sing alone, and was as successful as the real bird; besides, it was so much prettier to look at, for it sparkled like bracelets and breast pins. Three and thirty times did it sing the same tunes without being tired; the people would gladly have heard it again, but the emperor said the living nightingale ought to sing something. But where was she? No one had noticed her when she flew out at the open window, back to her own green woods.

"What strange conduct," said the emperor, when her flight had been discovered; and all the courtiers blamed her, and said she was a very ungrateful creature.

"But we have the best bird after all," said one, and then they would have the bird sing again, although it was the thirty-fourth time they had listened to the same piece, and even then they had not learned it, for it was rather difficult. But the music master praised the bird in the highest degree, and even asserted that it was better than a real nightingale, not only in its dress and the beautiful diamonds, but also in its musical power. "For you must perceive, my chief lord and emperor, that with a real nightingale we can never tell what is going to be sung, but with this bird everything is settled. It can be opened and explained, so that people may understand how the waltzes are formed, and why one note follows upon another."

"This is exactly what we think," they all replied, and then the music master received permission to exhibit the bird to the people on the following Sunday, and the emperor commanded that they should be present to hear it sing. When they heard it they were like people intoxicated; however it must have been with drinking tea, which is quite a Chinese custom. They all said "Oh!" and held up their forefingers and nodded, but a poor fisherman, who had heard the real nightingale, said, "It sounds prettily enough, and the melodies are all alike; yet there seems something wanting, I cannot exactly tell what."

And after this the real nightingale was banished from the empire, and the artificial bird placed on a silk cushion close to the emperor's bed. The presents of gold and precious stones which had been received with it were around the bird, and it was now advanced to the title of "Little Imperial Toilet Singer," and to the rank of number one on the left hand; for the emperor considered the left side, on which the heart lies, as the most noble, and the heart of an emperor is in the same place as that of other people.

The music master wrote a work, in twenty-five volumes, about the artificial bird, which was very learned and very long, and full of the most difficult Chinese words; yet all the people said they had read it, and understood it, for fear of being thought stupid and having their bodies trampled upon.

So a year passed, and the emperor, the court, and all the other Chinese knew every little turn in the artificial bird's song; and for that same reason it pleased them better. They could sing with the bird, which they often did. The street boys sang, "Zi-zi-zi, cluck, cluck, cluck," and the emperor himself could sing it also. It was really most amusing.

One evening, when the artificial bird was singing its best, and the emperor lay in bed listening to it, something inside the bird sounded "whizz." Then a spring cracked. "Whir-r-r-r" went all the wheels, running around, and then the music stopped. The emperor immediately sprang out of bed, and called for his physician; but what could he do? Then they sent for a watchmaker; and, after a great deal of talking and examination, the bird was put into something like order; but he said that it must be used very carefully, as the barrels were worn, and it would be impossible to put in new ones without injuring the music. Now there was great sorrow, as the bird could only be allowed to play once a year; and even that was dangerous for the works inside it. Then the music master made a little speech, full of hard words, and declared that the bird was as good as ever; and of course no one contradicted him.

Five years passed, and then a real grief came upon the land. The Chinese really were fond of their emperor, and he now lay so ill that he was not expected to live. Already a new emperor had been chosen and the people who stood in the street asked the lord-in-waiting how the old emperor was; but he only said, "Pooh!" and shook his head.

Cold and pale lay the emperor in his royal bed; the whole court thought he was dead, and everyone ran away to pay homage to his successor. The chamberlains went out to have a talk on the matter, and the ladies' maids invited company to take coffee. Cloth had been laid down on the halls and passages, so that not a footstep should be heard, and all was silent and still. But the emperor was not yet dead, although he lay white and stiff on his gorgeous bed, with the long velvet curtains and heavy gold tassels. A window stood open, and the moon shone in upon the emperor and the artificial bird. The poor emperor, finding he could scarcely breathe with a strange weight on his chest, opened his eyes, and saw Death sitting there. He had put on the emperor's golden crown, and held in one hand his sword of state, and in the other his beautiful banner. All around the bed and peeping through the long velvet curtains were a number of strange heads, some very ugly, and others lovely and gentle-looking. These were the emperor's good and bad deeds, which stared him in the face now that Death sat at his heart.

"Do you remember this?" "Do you recollect that?" they asked one after another, thus bringing to his remembrance circumstances that made perspiration stand on his brow.

"I know nothing about it," said the emperor. "Music! Music!" he cried. "The large Chinese drum! That I may not hear what they say." But they still went on, and Death nodded like a Chinaman to all they said. "Music! Music!" shouted the emperor. "You little precious golden bird, sing, pray sing! I have given you gold and costly presents; I have even hung my golden slipper around your neck. Sing! Sing!" But the bird remained silent. There was no one to wind it up, and therefore it could not sing a note.

Death continued to stare at the emperor with his cold, hollow eyes, and the room was fearfully still. Suddenly there came through the open window the sound of sweet music. Outside, on the bough of a tree, sat the living nightingale. She had heard of the emperor's illness, and was therefore come to sing to him of hope and trust. And as she sung, the

shadows grew paler and paler; the blood in the emperor's veins flowed more rapidly, and gave life to his weak limbs; and even Death himself listened, and said, "Go on, little nightingale, go on."

"Then will you give me the beautiful golden sword and that rich banner? And will you give me the emperor's crown?" said the bird.

So Death gave up each of these treasures for a song; and the nightingale continued her singing. She sung of the quiet churchyard, where the white roses grow, where the elder tree wafts its perfume on the breeze, and the fresh, sweet grass is moistened by the mourners' tears. Then Death longed to go and see his garden, and floated out through the window in the form of a cold, white mist.

"Thanks, thanks, you heavenly little bird. I know you well. I banished you from my kingdom once, and yet you have charmed away the evil faces from my bed, and banished Death from my heart, with your sweet song. How can I reward you?"

"You have already rewarded me," said the nightingale. "I shall never forget that I drew tears from your eyes the first time I sang to you. These are the jewels that rejoice a singer's heart. But now sleep, and grow strong and well again. I will sing to you again."

And as she sung, the emperor fell into a sweet sleep; and how mild and refreshing that slumber was! When he awoke, strengthened and restored, the sun shone brightly through the window; but not one of his servants had returned—they all believed he was dead; only the nightingale still sat beside him, and sang.

"You must always remain with me," said the emperor. "You shall sing only when it pleases you; and I will break the artificial bird into a thousand pieces."

"No; do not do that," replied the nightingale; "the bird did very well as long as it could. Keep it here still. I cannot live in the palace, and build my nest; but let me come when I like. I will sit on a bough outside your window, in the evening, and sing to you, so that you may be happy, and have thoughts full of joy. I will sing to you of those who are happy, and those who suffer; of the good and the evil, who are hidden around you. The little singing bird flies far from you and your court to the home of the fisherman and the peasant's cot. I love your heart better than your crown; and yet something holy lingers around that also. I will come, I will sing to you; but you must promise me one thing."

"Everything," said the emperor, who, having dressed himself in his imperial robes, stood with the hand that held the heavy golden sword pressed to his heart.

"I only ask one thing," she replied; "let no one know that you have a little bird who tells you everything. It will be best to conceal it." So saying, the nightingale flew away.

The servants now came in to look after the dead emperor; when, lo! there he stood, and, to their astonishment, said, "Good morning."

*She sat down and made a pair of little shoes out of some old pieces of red cloth.*

# THE RED SHOES

Once upon a time there was little girl, pretty and dainty. But in summertime she was obliged to go barefooted because she was poor, and in winter she had to wear large wooden shoes, so that her little instep grew quite red.

In the middle of the village lived an old shoemaker's wife; she sat down and made, as well as she could, a pair of little shoes out of some old pieces of red cloth. They were clumsy, but she meant well, for they were intended for the little girl, whose name was Karen.

Karen received the shoes and wore them for the first time on the day of her mother's funeral. They were certainly not suitable for mourning; but she had no others, and so she put her bare feet into them and walked behind the humble coffin.

Just then a large old carriage came by, and in it sat an old lady; she looked at the little girl, and taking pity on her, said to the clergyman, "Look here, if you will give me the little girl, I will take care of her."

Karen believed that this was all on account of the red shoes, but the old lady thought them hideous, and so they were burned. Karen herself was dressed very neatly and cleanly; she was taught to read and to sew, and people said that she was pretty. But the mirror told her, "You are more than pretty—you are beautiful."

One day the Queen was traveling through that part of the country, and had her little daughter, who was a princess, with her. All the people, among them Karen too, streamed towards the castle, where the little princess, in fine white clothes, stood before the window and allowed herself to be stared at. She wore neither a train nor a golden crown, but beautiful red morocco shoes; they were indeed much finer than those which the shoemaker's wife had sewn for little Karen. There is really nothing in the world that can be compared to red shoes!

Karen was now old enough to be confirmed; she received some new clothes, and she was also to have some new shoes. The rich shoemaker in the town took the measure of her little foot in his own room, in which there stood great glass cases full of pretty shoes and white slippers. It all looked very lovely, but the old lady could not see very well, and therefore did not get much pleasure out of it. Among the shoes stood a pair of red ones, like those which the princess had worn. How beautiful they were! And the shoemaker said that they had been made for a count's daughter, but that they had not fitted her.

"I suppose they are of shiny leather?" asked the old lady. "They shine so."

"Yes, they do shine," said Karen. They fitted her, and were bought. But the old lady knew nothing of their being red, for she would never have allowed Karen to be confirmed in red shoes, as she was now to be.

Everybody looked at her feet, and the whole of the way from the church door to the choir it seemed to her as if even the ancient figures on the monuments, in their stiff collars and long black robes, had their eyes fixed on her red shoes. It was only of these that she thought when the clergyman laid his hand upon her head and spoke of the holy baptism, of the covenant with God, and told her that she was now to be a grown-up Christian. The organ pealed forth solemnly, and the sweet children's voices mingled with that of their old leader; but Karen thought only of her red shoes. In the afternoon the old lady heard from everybody that Karen had worn red shoes. She said that it was a shocking thing to do, that it was very improper, and that Karen was always to go to church in future in black shoes, even if they were old.

On the following Sunday there was communion. Karen looked first at the black shoes, then at the red ones—looked at the red ones again, and put them on.

The sun was shining gloriously, so Karen and the old lady went along the footpath through the corn, where it was rather dusty.

At the church door stood an old crippled soldier leaning on a crutch; he had a wonderfully long beard, more red than white, and he bowed down to the ground and asked the old lady whether he might wipe her shoes. Then Karen put out her little foot too. "Dear me, what pretty dancing shoes!" said the soldier. "Sit fast, when you dance," said he, addressing the shoes, and slapping the soles with his hand.

The old lady gave the soldier some money and then went with Karen into the church.

And all the people inside looked at Karen's red shoes, and all the figures gazed at them; when Karen knelt before the altar and put the golden goblet to her mouth, she thought only of the red shoes. It seemed to her as though they were swimming about in the goblet, and she forgot to sing the psalm, forgot to say the Lord's Prayer.

Now everyone came out of church, and the old lady stepped into her carriage. But just as Karen was lifting up her foot to get in too, the old soldier said: "Dear me, what pretty dancing shoes!" and Karen could not help it, she was obliged to dance a few steps; and when she had once begun, her legs continued to dance. It seemed as if the shoes had got power over them. She danced around the church corner, for she could not stop; the coachman had to run after her and seize her. He lifted her into the carriage, but her feet continued to dance, so that she kicked the good old lady violently. At last they took off her shoes, and her legs were at rest.

At home the shoes were put into the cupboard, but Karen could not help looking at them.

Now the old lady fell ill, and it was said that she would not rise from her bed again. She had to be nursed and waited upon, and this was no one's duty more than Karen's. But there was a grand ball in the town, and Karen was invited. She looked at the red shoes, saying to herself that there was no sin in doing that; she put the red shoes on, thinking there was no harm in that either; and then she went to the ball; and commenced to dance.

But when she wanted to go to the right, the shoes danced to the left, and when she wanted to dance up the room, the shoes danced down the room, down the stairs through the street, and out through the gates of the town. She danced, and was obliged to dance, far out into the dark wood. Suddenly something shone up among the trees, and she believed it was the moon, for it was a face. But it was the old soldier with the red beard; he sat there nodding his head and said: "Dear me, what pretty dancing shoes!"

She was frightened, and wanted to throw the red shoes away; but they stuck fast. She tore off her stockings, but the shoes had grown fast to her feet. She danced and was obliged to go on dancing over field and meadow, in rain and sunshine, by night and by day—but by night it was most horrible.

She danced out into the open churchyard; but the dead there did not dance. They had something better to do than that. She wanted to sit down on the pauper's grave where the bitter fern grows; but for her there was neither peace nor rest. And as she danced past the open church door she saw an angel there in long white robes, with wings reaching from his shoulders down to the earth; his face was stern and grave, and in his hand he held a broad shining sword.

"Dance you shall," said he, "dance in your red shoes till you are pale and cold, till your skin shrivels up and you are a skeleton! Dance you shall, from door to door, and where proud and wicked children live you shall knock, so that they may hear you and fear you! Dance you shall, dance—!"

"Mercy!" cried Karen. But she did not hear what the angel answered, for the shoes carried her through the gate into the fields, along highways and byways, and unceasingly she had to dance.

One morning she danced past a door that she knew well; they were singing a psalm inside, and a coffin was being carried out covered with flowers. Then she knew that she was forsaken by everyone and damned by the angel of God.

She danced, and was obliged to go on dancing through the dark night. The shoes bore her away over thorns and stumps till she was all torn and bleeding; she danced away over the heath to a lonely little house. Here, she knew, lived the executioner; and she tapped with her finger at the window and said:

"Come out, come out! I cannot come in, for I must dance."

And the executioner said: "I don't suppose you know who I am. I strike off the heads of the wicked, and I notice that my axe is tingling to do so."

"Don't cut off my head!" said Karen. "For then I could not repent of my sin. But cut off my feet with the red shoes."

And then she confessed all her sin, and the executioner struck off her feet with the red shoes; but the shoes danced away with the little feet across the field into the deep forest.

And he carved her a pair of wooden feet and some crutches, and taught her a psalm which is always sung by sinners; she kissed the hand that guided the axe, and went away over the heath.

"Now, I have suffered enough for the red shoes," she said; "I will go to church, so that people can see me." And she went quickly up to the church door; but when she came there, the red shoes were dancing before her, and she was frightened, and turned back.

During the whole week she was sad and wept many bitter tears, but when Sunday came again she said: "Now I have suffered and striven enough. I believe I am quite as good as many of those who sit in church and give themselves airs." And so she went boldly on; but she had not got farther than the churchyard gate when she saw the red shoes dancing along before her. Then she became terrified, and turned back and repented right heartily of her sin.

She went to the parsonage, and begged that she might be taken into service there. She would be industrious, she said, and do everything that she could; she did not mind about the wages as long as she had a roof over her, and was with good people. The pastor's wife had pity on her, and took her into service. And she was industrious and thoughtful. She sat quiet and listened when the pastor read aloud from the Bible in the evening. All the children liked her very much, but when they spoke about dress and grandeur and beauty she would shake her head.

On the following Sunday they all went to church, and she was asked whether she wished to go too; but, with tears in her eyes, she looked sadly at her crutches. And then the others went to hear God's word, but she went alone into her little room; this was only large enough to hold the bed and a chair. Here she sat down with her hymn book, and as she was reading it with a pious mind, the wind carried the notes of the organ over to her from the church, and in tears she lifted up her face and said: "O God! Help me!"

Then the sun shone so brightly, and right before her stood an angel of God in white robes—it was the same one whom she had seen that night at the church door. He no longer carried the sharp sword but a beautiful green branch, full of roses; with this he touched the ceiling, which rose up very high, and where he had touched it there shone a golden star. He touched the walls, which opened wide apart, and she saw the organ which was pealing forth; she saw the pictures of the old pastors and their wives, and the congregation sitting in the polished chairs and singing from their hymn books. The church itself had come to the poor girl in her narrow room, or the room had gone to the church. She sat in the pew with the rest of the pastor's household, and when they had finished the hymn and looked up, they nodded and said, "It was right of you to come, Karen."

"It was mercy," said she.

The organ played and the children's voices in the choir sounded soft and lovely. The bright warm sunshine streamed through the window into the pew where Karen sat, and her heart became so filled with it, so filled with peace and joy, that it broke. Her soul flew on the sunbeams to heaven, and no one was there who asked after the red shoes.

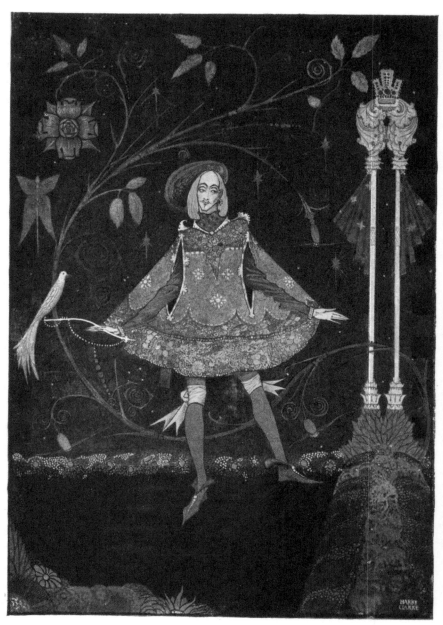

*On the grave of the prince's father grew a rose tree.*

# THE SWINEHERD

Once upon a time lived a poor prince; his kingdom was very small, but it was large enough to enable him to marry, and marry he would. It was rather bold of him to go and ask the emperor's daughter, "Will you marry me?" but he ventured to do so, for his name was known far and wide, and there were hundreds of princesses who would have gladly accepted him, but would she do so? Now we shall see.

On the grave of the prince's father grew a rose tree, the most beautiful of its kind. It bloomed only once in five years, and then it had only one single rose upon it, but what a rose! It had such a sweet scent that one instantly forgot all sorrow and grief when one smelled it. He had also a nightingale, which could sing as if every sweet melody was in its throat. This rose and the nightingale he wished to give to the princess; and therefore both were put into big silver cases and sent to her.

The emperor ordered them to be carried into the great hall where the princess was just playing "Visitors are coming" with her ladies-in-waiting; when she saw the large cases with the presents therein, she clapped her hands for joy.

"I wish it were a little pussy cat," she said. But then the rose tree with the beautiful rose was unpacked.

"Oh, how nicely it is made," exclaimed the ladies.

"It is more than nice," said the emperor, "it is charming."

The princess touched it and nearly began to cry.

"For shame, pa," she said, "it is not artificial, it is natural!"

"For shame, it is natural," repeated all her ladies.

"Let us first see what the other case contains before we are angry," said the emperor; then the nightingale was taken out, and it sang so beautifully that no one could possibly say anything unkind about it.

"*Superbe, charmant,*" said the ladies of the court, for they all prattled French, one worse than the other.

"How much the bird reminds me of the musical box of the late lamented empress," said an old courtier, "it has exactly the same tone, the same execution."

"You are right," said the emperor, and began to cry like a little child.

"I hope it is not natural," said the princess.

"Yes, certainly it is natural," replied those who had brought the presents.

"Then let it fly," said the princess, and refused to see the prince.

But the prince was not discouraged. He painted his face, put on common clothes, pulled his cap over his forehead, and came back.

"Good day, emperor," he said, "could you not give me some employment at the court?"

"There are so many," replied the emperor, "who apply for places, that for the present I have no vacancy, but I will remember you. But wait a moment; it just comes into my mind, I require somebody to look after my pigs, for I have a great many."

Thus the prince was appointed imperial swineherd, and as such he lived in a wretchedly small room near the pigsty; there he worked all day long, and when it was night he had made a pretty little pot. There were little bells around the rim, and when the water began to boil in it, the bells began to play the old tune:

> *"A jolly old sow once lived in a sty,*
> *Three little piggies has she,"* etc.

But what was more wonderful was that, when one put a finger into the steam rising from the pot, one could at once smell what meals they were preparing on every fire in the whole town. That was indeed much more remarkable than the rose. When the princess with her ladies passed by and heard the tune, she stopped and looked quite pleased, for she also could play it—in fact, it was the only tune she could play, and she played it with one finger.

"That is the tune I know," she exclaimed. "He must be a well-educated swineherd. Go and ask him how much the instrument is."

One of the ladies had to go and ask; but she put on clogs first.

"What will you take for your pot?" asked the lady.

"I will have ten kisses from the princess," said the swineherd.

"God forbid," said the lady.

"Well, I cannot sell it for less," replied the swineherd.

"What did he say?" said the princess.

"I really cannot tell you," replied the lady.

"You can whisper it into my ear."

"It is very naughty," said the princess, and walked off.

But when she had gone a little distance, the bells rang again so sweetly:

*"A jolly old sow once lived in a sty,*
*Three little piggies has she," etc.*

"Ask him," said the princess, "if he will be satisfied with ten kisses from one of my ladies."

"No, thank you," said the swineherd; "ten kisses from the princess, or I keep my pot."

"That is tiresome," said the princess. "But you must stand before me, so that nobody can see it."

The ladies placed themselves in front of her and spread out their dresses, and she gave the swineherd ten kisses and received the pot.

That was a pleasure! Day and night the water in the pot was boiling; there was not a single fire in the whole town of which they did not know what was preparing on it, the chamberlain's as well as the shoemaker's. The ladies danced and clapped their hands for joy.

"We know who will eat soup and pancakes; we know who will eat porridge and cutlets; oh, how interesting!"

"Very interesting, indeed," said the mistress of the household. "But you must not betray me, for I am the emperor's daughter."

"Of course not," they all said.

The swineherd (that is to say, the prince—but they did not know otherwise than that he was a real swineherd) did not waste a single day without doing something; he made a rattle, which, when turned quickly around, played all the waltzes, galops, and polkas known since the creation of the world.

"But that is superb," said the princess, passing by. "I have never heard a more beautiful composition. Go down and ask him what the instrument costs; but I shall not kiss him again."

"He will have a hundred kisses from the princess," said the lady, who had gone down to ask him.

"I believe he is mad," said the princess, and walked off, but soon she stopped. "One must encourage art," she said. "I am the emperor's daughter! Tell him I will give him ten kisses, as I did the other day; the remainder one of my ladies can give him.

"But we do not like to kiss him," said the ladies.

"That is nonsense," said the princess; "if I can kiss him, you can also do it. Remember that I give you food and employment." And the lady had to go down once more.

"A hundred kisses from the princess," said the swineherd, "or everybody keeps his own."

"Place yourselves before me," said the princess then. They did as they were bidden, and the princess kissed him.

"I wonder what that crowd near the pigsty means!" said the emperor, who had just come out on his balcony. He rubbed his eyes and put his spectacles on.

"The ladies of the court are up to some mischief, I think. I shall have to go down and see." He pulled up his shoes, for they were down at the heels, and he was very quick about it. When he had come down into the courtyard he walked quite softly, and the ladies were so busily engaged in counting the kisses, that all should be fair, that they did not notice the emperor. He raised himself on tiptoe.

*The ladies were so busily engaged in counting the kisses,*
*that they did not notice the emperor.*

"What does this mean?" he said, when he saw that his daughter was kissing the swineherd, and then hit their heads with his shoe just as the swineherd received the sixty-eighth kiss.

"Go out of my sight," said the emperor, for he was very angry; and both the princess and the swineherd were banished from the empire. There she stood and cried, the swineherd scolded her, and the rain came down in torrents.

"Alas, unfortunate creature that I am!" said the princess, "I wish I had accepted the prince. Oh, how wretched I am!"

The swineherd went behind a tree, wiped his face, threw off his poor attire, and stepped forth in his princely garments; he looked so beautiful that the princess could not help bowing to him.

"I have now learned to despise you," he said. "You refused an honest prince; you did not appreciate the rose and the nightingale; but you did not mind kissing a swineherd for his toys; you have no one but yourself to blame!"

And then he returned into his kingdom and left her behind. She could now sing at her leisure:

> *"A jolly old sow once lived in a sty,*
> *Three little piggies has she," etc.*

*"You refused an honest prince; but you did not mind kissing a swineherd for his toys."*

# THE UGLY DUCKLING

It was lovely summer weather in the country, and the golden corn, the green oats, and the haystacks piled up in the meadows looked beautiful. The stork walking about on his long red legs chattered in the Egyptian language, which he had learned from his mother. The cornfields and meadows were surrounded by large forests, in the midst of which were deep pools. It was, indeed, delightful to walk about in the country. In a sunny spot stood a pleasant old farmhouse close by a deep river, and from the house down to the water side grew great burdock leaves, so high that under the tallest of them a little child could stand upright. The spot was as wild as the center of a thick wood.

In this snug retreat sat a duck on her nest, watching for her young brood to hatch; she was beginning to get tired of her task, for the little ones were a long time coming out of their shells, and she seldom had any visitors. The other ducks liked much better to swim about in the river than to climb the slippery banks, and sit under a burdock leaf, to have a gossip with her. At length one shell cracked, and then another, and from each egg came a living creature that lifted its head and cried, "Peep, peep." "Quack, quack," said the mother, and then they all quacked as well as they could, and looked about them on every side at the large green leaves. Their mother allowed them to look as much as they liked, because green is good for the eyes. "How large the world is," said the young ducks, when they found how much more room they now had than while they were inside the eggshell. "Do you imagine this is the whole world?" asked the mother. "Wait till you have seen the garden; it stretches far beyond that to the parson's field, but I have never ventured to such a distance. Are you all out?" she continued, rising; "No, I declare, the largest egg lies there still. I wonder how long this is to last. I am quite tired of it," and she seated herself again on the nest.

"Well, how are you getting on?" asked an old duck, who paid her a visit.

"One egg is not hatched yet," said the duck, "it will not break. But just look at all the others, are they not the prettiest little ducklings you ever saw? They are the image of their father, who is so unkind, he never comes to see."

"Let me see the egg that will not break," said the duck; "I have no doubt it is a turkey's egg. I was persuaded to hatch some once, and after all my care and trouble with the young ones, they were afraid of the water. I quacked and clucked, but all to no purpose. I could not get them to venture in. Let me look at the egg. Yes, that is a turkey's egg; take my advice, leave it where it is and teach the other children to swim."

"I think I will sit on it a little while longer," said the duck; "as I have sat so long already, a few days will be nothing."

"Please yourself," said the old duck, and she went away.

At last the large egg broke, and a young one crept forth crying, "Peep, peep." It was very large and ugly. The duck stared at it and exclaimed, "It is very large and not at all like the others. I wonder if it really is a turkey. We shall soon find out, however, when we go to the water. It must go in, if I have to push it myself."

On the next day the weather was delightful, and the sun shone brightly on the green burdock leaves, so the mother duck took her young brood down to the water, and jumped in with a splash. "Quack, quack," cried she, and one after another the little ducklings jumped in. The water closed over their heads, but they came up again in an instant, and swam about quite prettily with their legs paddling under them as easily as possible, and the ugly duckling was also in the water swimming with them.

"Oh," said the mother, "that is not a turkey; how well he uses his legs, and how upright he holds himself! He is my own child, and he is not so very ugly after all if you look at him properly. Quack, quack! Come with me now, I will take you into grand society, and introduce you to the farmyard, but you must keep close to me or you may be trodden upon; and, above all, beware of the cat."

When they reached the farmyard, there was a great disturbance—two families were fighting for an eel's head, which, after all, was carried off by the cat. "See, children, that is the way of the world," said the mother duck, whetting her beak, for she would have liked the eel's head herself. "Come, now, use your legs, and let me see how well you can behave. You must bow your heads prettily to that old duck yonder; she is the highest born of them all, and has Spanish blood, therefore, she is well off. Don't you see she has a red flag tied to her leg, which is something very grand, and a great honor for a duck; it shows that everyone is anxious not to lose her, as she can be recognized both by man and beast. Come, now, don't turn your toes, a well-bred duckling spreads his feet wide apart, just like his father and mother, in this way; now bend your neck, and say 'quack.'"

The ducklings did as they were bid, but the other duck stared, and said, "Look, here comes another brood, as if there were not enough of us already! And what a queer-looking object one of them is; we don't want him here," and then one flew out and bit him in the neck.

"Let him alone," said the mother; "he is not doing any harm."

"Yes, but he is so big and ugly," said the spiteful duck, "and therefore he must be turned out."

"The others are very pretty children," said the old duck, with the rag on her leg, "all but that one; I wish his mother could improve him a little."

"That is impossible, your grace," replied the mother; "he is not pretty; but he has a very good disposition, and swims as well or even better than the others. I think he will grow up pretty, and perhaps be smaller; he has remained too long in the egg, and therefore his figure is not properly formed"; and then she stroked his neck and smoothed the feathers, saying, "It is a drake, and therefore not of so much consequence. I think he will grow up strong, and able to take care of himself."

"The other ducklings are graceful enough," said the old duck. "Now make yourself at home, and if you can find an eel's head, you can bring it to me."

And so they made themselves comfortable; but the poor duckling, who had crept out of his shell last of all, and looked so ugly, was bitten and pushed and made fun of, not only by the ducks, but by all the poultry. "He is too big," they all said, and the turkey cock, who had been born into the world with spurs, and fancied himself really an emperor, puffed himself out like a vessel in full sail, and flew at the duckling, and became quite red in the head with passion, so that the poor little thing did not know where to go, and was quite miserable because he was so ugly and laughed at by the whole farmyard. So it went on from day to day till it got worse and worse. The poor duckling was driven about by everyone; even his brothers and sisters were unkind to him, and would say, "Ah, you ugly creature, I wish the cat would get you," and his mother said she wished he had never been born. The ducks pecked him, the chickens beat him, and the girl who fed the poultry kicked him with her feet. So at last he ran away, frightening the little birds in the hedge as he flew over the palings.

"They are afraid of me because I am ugly," he said. So he closed his eyes, and flew still farther, until he came out on a large moor, inhabited by wild ducks. Here he remained the whole night, feeling very tired and sorrowful.

In the morning, when the wild ducks rose in the air, they stared at their new comrade. "What sort of a duck are you?" they all said, coming around him.

He bowed to them, and was as polite as he could be, but he did not reply to their question.

"You are exceedingly ugly," said the wild ducks, "but that will not matter if you do not want to marry one of our family."

Poor thing! He had no thoughts of marriage; all he wanted was permission to lie among the rushes, and drink some of the water on the

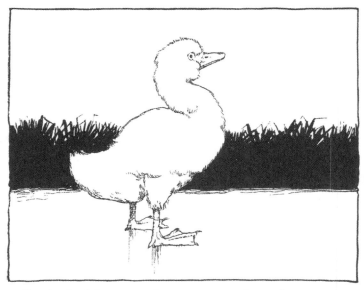

moor. After he had been on the moor two days, there came two wild geese, or rather goslings, for they had not been out of the egg long, and were very saucy. "Listen, friend," said one of them to the duckling, "you are so ugly, that we like you very well. Will you go with us, and become a bird of passage? Not far from here is another moor, in which there are some pretty wild geese, all unmarried. It is a chance for you to get a wife; you may be lucky, ugly as you are."

"Pop, pop," sounded in the air, and the two wild geese fell dead among the rushes, and the water was tinged with blood. "Pop, pop," echoed far and wide in the distance, and whole flocks of wild geese rose up from the rushes. The sound continued from every direction, for the sportsmen surrounded the moor, and some were even seated on branches of trees, overlooking the rushes. The blue smoke from the guns rose like clouds over the dark trees, and as it floated away across the water, a number of sporting dogs bounded in among the rushes, which bent beneath them wherever they went. How they terrified the poor duckling! He turned away his head to hide it under his wing, and at the same moment a large terrible dog passed quite near him. His jaws were open, his tongue hung from his mouth, and his eyes glared fearfully. He thrust his nose close to the duckling, showing his sharp teeth, and then, "splash, splash," he went into the water without touching him, "Oh," sighed the duckling, "how thankful I am for being so ugly; even a dog will not bite me." And so he lay quite still, while the shot rattled through the rushes, and gun after gun was fired over him.

It was late in the day before all became quiet, but even then the poor young thing did not dare to move. He waited quietly for several hours, and then, after looking carefully around him, hastened away from the moor as fast as he could. He ran over field and meadow till a storm arose, and he could hardly struggle against it. Towards evening, he reached a poor little cottage that seemed ready to fall, and only remained standing because it could not decide on which side to fall first. The storm continued so violently that the duckling could go no farther; he sat down by the cottage, and then he noticed that the door was not quite closed in consequence of one of the hinges having given way. There was therefore a narrow opening near the bottom large enough for him to slip through, which he did very quietly, and got a shelter for the night.

A woman, a tomcat, and a hen lived in this cottage. The tomcat, whom the mistress called "My little son," was a great favorite; he could raise his back and purr, and could even throw out sparks from his fur if it were stroked the wrong way. The hen had very short legs, so she was called "Chickie short legs." She laid good eggs, and her mistress loved her as if she had been her own child. In the morning, the strange visitor was discovered, and the tomcat began to purr, and the hen to cluck.

"What is that noise about?" said the old woman, looking around the room, but her sight was not very good; therefore, when she saw the duckling she thought it must be a fat duck that had strayed from home. "Oh, what a prize!" she exclaimed. "I hope it is not a drake, for then I shall have some duck's eggs. I must wait and see." So the duckling was allowed to remain on trial for three weeks, but there were no eggs.

Now the tomcat was the master of the house, and the hen was mistress, and they always said, "We and the world," for they believed themselves to be half the world, and the better half too. The duckling thought that others might hold a different opinion on the subject, but the hen would not listen to such doubts. "Can you lay eggs?" she asked. "No." "Then have the goodness to hold your tongue." "Can you raise your back, or purr, or throw out sparks?" said the tomcat. "No." "Then you have no right to express an opinion when sensible people are speaking." So the duckling sat in a corner, feeling very low-spirited, till the sunshine and the fresh air came into the room through the open door, and then he began to  feel such a great longing for a swim on the water, that he could not help telling the hen.

"What an absurd idea," said the hen. "You have nothing else to do, therefore you have foolish fancies. If you could purr or lay eggs, they would pass away."

"But it is so delightful to swim about on the water," said the duckling, "and so refreshing to feel it close over your head, while you dive down to the bottom."

"Delightful, indeed!" said the hen. "Why, you must be crazy! Ask the cat, he is the cleverest animal I know, ask him how he would like to swim about on the water, or to dive under it, for I will not speak of my own opinion; ask our mistress, the old woman—there is no one in the world cleverer than she is. Do you think she would like to swim, or to let the water close over her head?"

"You don't understand me," said the duckling.

"We don't understand you? Who can understand you, I wonder? Do you consider yourself cleverer than the cat, or the old woman? I will say nothing of myself. Don't imagine such nonsense, child, and thank your good fortune that you have been received here. Are you not in a warm room, and in society from which you may learn something? But you are a chatterer, and your company is not very agreeable. Believe me, I speak only for your own good. I may tell you unpleasant truths, but that is a proof of my friendship. I advise you, therefore, to lay eggs, and learn to purr as quickly as possible."

"I believe I must go out into the world again," said the duckling.

"Yes, do," said the hen. So the duckling left the cottage, and soon found water on which it could swim and dive, but was avoided by all other animals, because of its ugly appearance. Autumn came, and the leaves in the forest turned to orange and gold. Then, as winter approached, the wind caught them as they fell and whirled them in the cold air. The clouds, heavy with hail and snowflakes, hung low in the sky, and the raven stood on the ferns crying, "Croak, croak." It made one shiver with cold to look at him. All this was very sad for the poor little duckling. One evening, just as the sun set amid radiant clouds, there came a large flock of beautiful birds out of the bushes. The duckling had never seen any like them before. They were swans, and they curved their graceful necks, while their soft plumage shone with dazzling whiteness. They uttered a singular cry, as they spread their glorious wings and flew away from those cold regions to warmer countries across the sea.

As they mounted higher and higher in the air, the ugly little duckling felt quite a strange sensation as he watched them. He whirled himself in the water like a wheel, stretched out his neck towards them, and uttered a cry so strange that it frightened himself. Could he ever forget those beautiful, happy birds? And when at last they were out of his sight, he dived under the water, and rose again almost beside himself with excitement. He knew not the names of these birds, nor where they had flown, but he felt towards them as he had never felt for any other bird in the world. He was not envious of these beautiful creatures, but wished to be as lovely as they. Poor ugly creature, how gladly he would have lived even with the ducks had they only given him encouragement.

The winter grew colder and colder; he was obliged to swim about on the water to keep it from freezing, but every night the space on which he swam became smaller and smaller. At length it froze so hard that the ice in the water crackled as he moved, and the duckling had to paddle with his legs as well as he could, to keep the space from closing up. He became exhausted at last, and lay still and helpless, frozen fast in the ice.

Early in the morning, a peasant, who was passing by, saw what had happened. He broke the ice in pieces with his wooden shoe, and carried the duckling home to his wife. The warmth revived the poor little creature; but when the children wanted to play with him, the duckling thought they would do him some harm; so he started up in terror, fluttered into the milk pan, and splashed the milk about the room. Then the woman clapped her hands, which frightened him still more. He flew first into the butter cask, then into the meal tub, and out again. What a condition he was in! The woman screamed, and struck at him with the tongs; the children laughed and screamed, and tumbled over each other in their efforts to catch him; but luckily he escaped. The door stood open; the poor creature could just manage to slip out among the bushes, and lie down quite exhausted in the newly fallen snow.

It would be very sad, were I to relate all the misery and privations which the poor little duckling endured during the hard winter; but when it had passed, he found himself lying one morning in a moor, among the rushes. He felt the warm sun shining, and heard the lark singing, and saw that all around was beautiful spring. Then the young bird felt that his wings were strong, as he flapped them against his sides, and rose high into the air. They bore him onwards, until he found himself in a large garden, before he well knew how it had happened. The apple trees were in full blossom, and the fragrant elders bent their long green branches down to the stream which wound around a smooth lawn. Everything looked beautiful in the freshness of early spring. From a thicket close by came three beautiful white swans, rustling their feathers, and swimming lightly over the smooth water. The duckling remembered the lovely birds, and felt more strangely unhappy than ever.

"I will fly to those royal birds," he exclaimed, "and they will kill me, because I am so ugly, and dare to approach them; but it does not matter. Better to be killed by them than pecked by the ducks, beaten by the hens, pushed about by the maiden who feeds the poultry, or starved with hunger in the winter."

Then he flew to the water, and swam towards the beautiful swans. The moment they espied the stranger, they rushed to meet him with outstretched wings.

"Kill me," said the poor bird; and he bent his head down to the surface of the water, and awaited death.

But what did he see in the clear stream below? His own image; no longer a dark, gray bird, ugly and disagreeable to look at, but a graceful and beautiful swan. To be born in a duck's nest, in a farmyard, is of no consequence to a bird, if it is hatched from a swan's egg. He now felt glad at having suffered sorrow and trouble, because it enabled him to enjoy so much better all the pleasure and happiness around him; for the great swans swam around the newcomer, and stroked his neck with their beaks, as a welcome.

Into the garden presently came some little children, and threw bread and cake into the water.

"See," cried the youngest, "there is a new one"; and the rest were delighted, and ran to their father and mother, dancing and clapping their hands, and shouting joyously, "There is another swan come; a new one has arrived."

Then they threw more bread and cake into the water, and said, "The new one is the most beautiful of all; he is so young and pretty." And the old swans bowed their heads before him.

Then he felt quite ashamed, and hid his head under his wing, for he did not know what to do: he was so happy, and yet not at all proud. He had been persecuted and despised for his ugliness, and now he heard them say he was the most beautiful of all the birds. Even the elder tree bent down its bows into the water before him, and the sun shone warm and bright. Then he rustled his feathers, curved his slender neck, and cried joyfully, from the depths of his heart, "I never dreamed of such happiness as this while I was an ugly duckling."

*The roses and the hymn book told the real truth.*

# THE WILD SWANS

Far away in the land to which the swallows fly when it is winter dwelt a king who had eleven sons, and one daughter, named Eliza. The eleven brothers were princes, and each went to school with a star on his breast, and a sword by his side. They wrote with diamond pencils on gold slates, and learned their lessons so quickly and read so easily that everyone might know they were princes. Their sister Eliza sat on a little stool of plate glass, and had a book full of pictures, which had cost as much as half a kingdom. Oh, these children were indeed happy, but it was not to remain so always. Their father, who was king of the country, married a very wicked queen, who did not love the poor children at all. They knew this from the very first day after the wedding. In the palace there were great festivities, and the children played at receiving company; but instead of having, as usual, all the cakes and apples that were left, she gave them some sand in a teacup, and told them to pretend it was cake. The week after, she sent little Eliza into the country to a peasant and his wife, and then she told the king so many untrue things about the young princes, that he gave himself no more trouble respecting them.

"Go out into the world and get your own living," said the queen. "Fly like great birds, who have no voice." But she could not make them ugly as she wished, for they were turned into eleven beautiful wild swans. Then, with a strange cry, they flew through the windows of the palace, over the park, to the forest beyond. It was early morning when they passed the peasant's cottage, where their sister Eliza lay asleep in her room. They hovered over the roof, twisted their long necks, and flapped their wings, but no one heard them or saw them, so they were at last obliged to fly away, high up in the clouds; and over the wide world they flew till they came to a thick, dark wood, which stretched far away to the seashore. Poor little Eliza was alone in her room playing with a green leaf, for she had no other playthings, and she pierced a hole through the leaf, and looked through it at the sun, and it was as if she saw her brothers' clear eyes, and when the warm sun shone on her cheeks, she thought of all the kisses they had given her. One day passed just like another; sometimes the winds rustled through the leaves of the rosebush, and would whisper to the roses, "Who can be more beautiful than you!" But the roses would shake their heads and say, "Eliza is." And when the old woman sat at the cottage door on Sunday and read her hymn book, the wind would flutter the leaves and say to the book, "Who can be more pious than you?" and then the hymn book would answer, "Eliza." And the roses and the hymn book told the real truth.

At fifteen she returned home, but when the queen saw how beautiful she was, she became full of spite and hatred towards her. Willingly would she have turned her into a swan, like her brothers, but she did not dare to do so yet, because the king wished to see his daughter. Early one morning the queen went into the bathroom; it was built of marble, and had soft cushions, trimmed with the most beautiful tapestry. She took three toads with her, and kissed them, and said to one, "When Eliza comes to the bath, seat yourself upon her head, that she may become as stupid as you are." Then she said to another, "Place yourself on her forehead, that she may become as ugly as you are, and that her father may not know her." "Rest on her heart," she whispered to the third, "then she will have evil inclinations, and suffer in consequence." So she put the toads into the clear water, and they turned green immediately.

She next called Eliza, and helped her to undress and get into the bath. As Eliza dipped her head under the water, one of the toads sat on her hair, a second on her forehead, and a third on her breast, but she did not seem to notice them, and when she rose out of the water, there were three red poppies floating upon it. Had not the creatures been venomous or been kissed by the witch, they would have been changed into red roses. In any event they became flowers, because they had rested on Eliza's head, and on her heart. She was too good and too innocent for witchcraft to have any power over her. When the wicked queen saw this, she rubbed her face with walnut juice, so that she was quite brown; then she tangled her beautiful hair and smeared it with disgusting ointment, till it was quite impossible to recognize the beautiful Eliza.

When her father saw her, he was much shocked, and declared she was not his daughter. No one but the watchdog and the swallows knew her; and they were only poor animals, and could say nothing. Then poor Eliza wept, and thought of her eleven brothers, who were all away. Sorrowfully, she stole away from the palace, and walked, the whole day, over fields and moors, till she came to the great forest. She knew not in what direction to go; but she was so unhappy, and longed so for her brothers, who had been, like herself, driven out into the world, that she was determined to seek them. She had been but a short time in the wood when night came on, and she quite lost the path; so she laid herself down on the soft moss, offered up her evening prayer, and leaned her head against the stump of a tree. All nature was still, and the soft, mild air fanned her forehead. The light of hundreds of glowworms shone amid the grass and the moss, like green fire; and if she touched a twig with her hand, ever so lightly, the brilliant insects fell down around her, like shooting stars.

All night long she dreamed of her brothers. She and they were children again, playing together. She saw them writing with their diamond pencils on golden slates, while she looked at the beautiful picture book which had cost half a kingdom. They were not writing lines and letters, as they used to do; but descriptions of the noble deeds they had performed, and of all they had discovered and seen. In the picture book, too, everything was living. The birds sang, and the people came out of the book, and spoke to Eliza and her brothers; but, as the leaves turned over, they darted back again to their places, that all might be in order.

When she awoke, the sun was high in the heavens; yet she could not see him, for the lofty trees spread their branches thickly over her head; but his beams were glancing through the leaves here and there, like a golden mist. There was a sweet fragrance from the fresh green verdure, and the birds almost perched upon her shoulders. She heard water rippling from a number of springs, all flowing in a lake with golden sands. Bushes grew thickly around the lake, and at one spot an opening had been made by a deer, through which Eliza went down to the water. The lake was so clear that, had not the wind rustled the branches of the trees and the bushes so that they moved, they would have appeared as if painted in the depths of the lake; for every leaf was reflected in the water, whether it stood in the shade or the sunshine. As soon as Eliza saw her own face, she was quite terrified at finding it so brown and ugly; but when she wetted her little hand, and rubbed her eyes and forehead, the white skin gleamed forth once more; and, after she had undressed and dipped herself in the fresh water, a more beautiful king's daughter could not be found in the wide world.

As soon as she had dressed herself again and braided her long hair, she went to the bubbling spring and drank some water out of the hollow of her hand. Then she wandered far into the forest, not knowing whither she went. She thought of her brothers, and felt sure that God would not forsake her. It is God who makes the wild apples grow in the wood, to satisfy the hungry, and he now led her to one of these trees, which was so loaded with fruit that the boughs bent beneath the weight. Here she held her noonday repast, placed props under the boughs, and then went into the gloomiest depths of the forest. It was so still that she could hear the sound of her own footsteps, as well as the rustling of every withered leaf which she crushed under her feet. Not a bird was to be seen, not a sunbeam could penetrate through the large, dark boughs of the trees. Their lofty trunks stood so close together that, when she looked before her, it seemed as if she were enclosed within trelliswork. Such solitude she had never known before. The night was very dark. Not a single glowworm glittered in the moss.

Sorrowfully she laid herself down to sleep; and, after a while, it seemed to her as if the branches of the trees parted over her head, and that the mild eyes of angels looked down upon her from heaven. When she awoke in the morning, she knew not whether she had dreamed this, or if it had really been so. Then she continued her wandering; but she had not gone many steps forward when she met an old woman with berries in her basket, who gave her a few to eat. Then Eliza asked her if she had not seen eleven princes riding through the forest.

"No," replied the old woman, "But I saw yesterday eleven swans, with gold crowns on their heads, swimming on the river close by." Then she led Eliza a little distance farther to a sloping bank, and at the foot of it wound a little river. The trees on its banks stretched their long leafy branches across the water towards each other, and where the growth prevented them from meeting naturally, the roots had torn themselves away from the ground, so that the branches might mingle their foliage as they hung over the water.

Eliza bade the old woman farewell, and walked by the flowing river, till she reached the shore of the open sea. And there, before the young maiden's eyes, lay the glorious ocean, but not a sail appeared on its surface, not even a boat could be seen. How was she to go farther?

She noticed how the countless pebbles on the seashore had been smoothed and rounded by the action of the water. Glass, iron, stones, everything that lay there mingled together, had taken its shape from the same power, and felt as smooth, or even smoother than her own delicate hand. "The water rolls on without weariness," she said, "till all that is hard becomes smooth; so will I be unwearied in my task. Thanks for your lessons, bright rolling waves; my heart tells me you will lead me to my dear brothers." On the foam-covered seaweeds lay eleven white swan feathers, which she gathered up and placed together. Drops of water lay upon them; whether they were dewdrops or tears no one could say. Lonely as it was on the seashore, she did not notice it, for the ever-moving sea showed more changes in a few hours than the most varying lake could produce during a whole year. If a black heavy cloud arose, it was as if the sea said, "I can look dark and angry too"; and then the wind blew, and the waves turned to white foam as they rolled. When the wind slept and the clouds glowed with the red sunlight, then the sea looked like a rose leaf. But however quietly its white glassy surface rested, there was still a motion on the shore, as its waves rose and fell like the breast of a sleeping child.

When the sun was about to set, Eliza saw eleven white swans with golden crowns on their heads flying towards the land, one behind the other, like a long white ribbon. Then Eliza went down the slope from the shore, and hid herself behind the bushes. The swans alighted quite close to her and flapped their great white wings. As soon as the sun had disappeared under the water, the feathers of the swans fell off, and eleven beautiful princes, Eliza's brothers, stood near her. She uttered a loud cry, for, although they were very much changed, she knew them immediately. She sprang into their arms and called them each by name. Then how happy the princes were at meeting their little sister again, for they recognized her, although she had grown so tall and beautiful. They laughed and they wept, and very soon understood how wickedly their mother had acted to them all.

"We brothers," said the eldest, "fly about as wild swans, so long as the sun is in the sky; but as soon as it sinks behind the hills, we recover our human shape. Therefore must we always be near a resting place for our feet before sunset; for if we should be flying towards the clouds at the time we recovered our natural shape as men, we should sink deep into the sea. We do not dwell here, but in a land just as fair that lies beyond the ocean, which we have to cross for a long distance; there is no island in our passage upon which we could pass the night; nothing but a little rock rising out of the sea, upon which we can scarcely stand with safety, even closely crowded together. If the sea is rough, the foam dashes over us, yet we thank God even for this rock; we have passed whole nights upon it, or we should never have reached our beloved fatherland, for our flight across the sea occupies two of the longest days in the year.

"We have permission to visit our home once in every year, and to remain eleven days, during which we fly across the forest to look once more at the palace where our father dwells, and where we were born, and at the church where our mother lies buried. Here it seems as if the very trees and bushes were related to us. The wild horses leap over the plains as we have seen them in our childhood. The charcoal burners sing the old songs, to which we have danced as children. This is our fatherland, to which we are drawn by loving ties; and here we have found you, our dear little sister. Two days longer we can remain here, and then must we fly away to a beautiful land which is not our home; and how can we take you with us? We have neither ship nor boat."

"How can I break this spell?" said their sister. And then she talked about it nearly the whole night, only slumbering for a few hours. Eliza was awakened by the rustling of the swans' wings as they soared above. Her brothers were again changed to swans, and they flew in circles wider and wider, till they were far away; but one of them, the youngest swan, remained behind, and laid his head in his sister's lap while she stroked his wings; and they remained together the whole day. Towards evening the rest came back, and as the sun went down they resumed their natural forms. "Tomorrow," said one, "we shall fly away, not to return again till a whole year has passed. But we cannot leave you here. Have you courage to go with us? My arm is strong enough to carry you through the wood; and will not all our wings be strong enough to fly with you over the sea?"

"Yes, take me with you," said Eliza. Then they spent the whole night in weaving a net with the pliant willow and rushes. It was very large and strong. Eliza laid herself down on the net, and when the sun rose, and her brothers again became wild swans, they took up the net with their beaks, and flew up to the clouds with their dear sister, who still slept. The sunbeams fell on her face, therefore one of the swans soared over her head, so that his broad wings might shade her. They were far from the land when Eliza woke. She thought she must still be dreaming, it seemed so strange to her to feel herself being carried so high in the air over the sea. By her side lay a branch full of beautiful ripe berries, and a bundle of sweet roots; the youngest of her brothers had gathered them for her, and placed them by her side. She smiled her thanks to him; she knew it was the same who had hovered over her to shade her with his wings.

They were now so high that a large ship beneath them looked like a white seagull skimming the waves. A great cloud floating behind them appeared like a vast mountain, and upon it Eliza saw her own shadow and those of the eleven swans, looking gigantic in size. Altogether it formed a more beautiful picture than she had ever seen; but as the sun rose higher and the clouds were left behind, the shadowy picture vanished away.

Onward the whole day they flew through the air like a winged arrow, yet more slowly than usual, for they had their sister to carry. The weather seemed inclined to be stormy, and Eliza watched the sinking sun with great anxiety, for the little rock in the ocean was not yet in sight. It appeared to her as if the swans were making great efforts with their wings. Alas! She was the cause of their not advancing more quickly. When the sun set, they would change to men, fall into the sea, and be drowned. Then she offered a prayer from her inmost heart, but still no appearance of the rock. Dark clouds came nearer, the gusts of wind told of a coming storm, while from a thick, heavy mass of clouds the lightning burst forth flash after flash. The sun had reached the edge of the sea when the swans darted down so swiftly that Eliza's head trembled; she believed they were falling, but they again soared onward.

Presently she caught sight of the rock just below them, and by this time the sun was half hidden by the waves. The rock did not appear larger than a seal's head thrust out of the water. They sunk so rapidly, that at the moment their feet touched the rock, it shone only like a star, and at last disappeared like the last spark in a piece of burned paper. Then she saw her brothers standing closely around her with their arms linked together. There was but just room enough for them, and not the smallest space to spare. The sea dashed against the rock and covered them with spray. The heavens were lighted up with continual flashes,

*They took up the net with their beaks, and flew up to the clouds
with their dear sister.*

and peal after peal of thunder rolled. But the sister and brothers sat holding each other's hands and singing hymns, from which they gained hope and courage.

In the early dawn the air became calm and still, and at sunrise the swans flew away from the rock with Eliza. The sea was still rough, and from their high position in the air, the white foam on the dark green waves looked like millions of swans swimming on the water. As the sun rose higher, Eliza saw before her, floating on the air, a range of mountains, with shining masses of ice on their summits. In the center rose a castle apparently a mile long, with rows of columns rising one above another, while, around it, palm trees waved and flowers bloomed as large as mill wheels. She asked if this was the land to which they were hastening. The swans shook their heads, for what she beheld were the beautiful ever-changing cloud palaces of the "Fata Morgana," into which no mortal can enter.

Eliza was still gazing at the scene when mountains, forests, and castles melted away, and twenty stately churches rose in their stead, with high towers and pointed gothic windows. Eliza even fancied she could hear the tones of the organ, but it was the music of the murmuring sea which she heard. As they drew nearer to the churches, they also changed into a fleet of ships, which seemed to be sailing beneath her; but as she looked again, she found it was only a sea mist gliding over the ocean. So there continued to pass before her eyes a constant change of scene, till at last she saw the real land to which they were bound, with its blue mountains, its cedar forests, and its cities and palaces. Long before the sun went down, she sat on a rock in front of a large cave, on the floor of which the overgrown yet delicate green creeping plants looked like an embroidered carpet. "Now we shall expect to hear what you dream of tonight," said the youngest brother, as he showed his sister her bedroom.

"Heaven grant that I may dream how to save you," she replied. And this thought took such hold upon her mind that she prayed earnestly to God for help, and even in her sleep she continued to pray. Then it appeared to her as if she were flying high in the air, towards the cloudy palace of the "Fata Morgana," and a fairy came out to meet her, radiant and beautiful in appearance, and yet very much like the old woman who had given her berries in the wood, and who had told her of the swans with golden crowns on their heads.

"Your brothers can be released," said she, "if you have only courage and perseverance. True, water is softer than your own delicate hands, and yet it polishes stones into shapes; it feels no pain as your fingers would feel, it has no soul, and cannot suffer such agony and torment as you will have to endure. Do you see the stinging nettle which I hold in my hand? Quantities of the same sort grow around the cave in which you sleep, but none will be of any use to you unless they grow upon the graves in a churchyard. These you must gather even while they burn blisters on your hands. Break them to pieces with your hands and feet, and they will become flax, from which you must spin and weave eleven coats with long sleeves; if these are then thrown over the eleven swans, the spell will be broken. But remember that from the moment you commence your task until it is finished, even should it occupy years of your life, you must not speak. The first word you utter will pierce through the hearts of your brothers like a deadly dagger. Their lives hang upon your tongue. Remember all I have told you." And as she finished speaking, she touched her hand lightly with the nettle, and a pain, as of burning fire, awoke Eliza.

It was broad daylight, and close by where she had been sleeping lay a nettle like the one she had seen in her dream. She fell on her knees and offered her thanks to God. Then she went forth from the cave to begin her work with her delicate hands. She groped in among the ugly nettles, which burned great blisters on her hands and arms, but she determined to bear it gladly if she could only release her dear brothers. So she bruised the nettles with her bare feet and spun the flax.

At sunset her brothers returned and were very much frightened when they found her dumb. They believed it to be some new sorcery of their wicked stepmother. But when they saw her hands they understood what she was doing on their behalf, and the youngest brother wept, and where his tears fell the pain ceased, and the burning blisters vanished. She kept to her work all night, for she could not rest till she had released her dear brothers.

During the whole of the following day, while her brothers were absent, she sat in solitude, but never before had the time flown so quickly. One coat was already finished and she had begun the second, when she heard the huntsman's horn, and was struck with fear. The sound came nearer and nearer, she heard the dogs barking, and fled with terror into the cave. She hastily bound together the nettles she had gathered into a bundle and sat upon them. Immediately a great dog came bounding towards her out of the ravine, and then another and another; they barked loudly, ran back, and then came again. In a very few minutes all the huntsmen stood before the cave, and the handsomest of them was the king of the country. He advanced towards her, for he had never seen a more beautiful maiden.

"How did you come here, my sweet child?" he asked. But Eliza shook her head. She dared not speak, at the cost of her brothers' lives. And she hid her hands under her apron, so that the king might not see how she must be suffering.

"Come with me," he said; "here you cannot remain. If you are as good as you are beautiful, I will dress you in silk and velvet, I will place a golden crown upon your head, and you shall dwell, and rule, and make your home in my richest castle." And then he lifted her on his horse. She wept and wrung her hands, but the king said, "I wish only for your happiness. A time will come when you will thank me for this." And then he galloped away over the mountains, holding her before him on this horse, and the hunters followed behind them.

As the sun went down, they approached a fair royal city with churches and cupolas. On arriving at the castle the king led her into marble halls, where large fountains played, and where the walls and the ceilings were covered with rich paintings. But she had no eyes for all these glorious sights, she could only mourn and weep. Patiently she allowed the women to array her in royal robes, to weave pearls in her hair, and draw soft gloves over her blistered fingers. As she stood before them in all her rich dress, she looked so dazzlingly beautiful that the court bowed low in her presence. Then the king declared his intention of making her his bride, but the archbishop shook his head, and whispered that the fair young maiden was only a witch who had blinded the king's eyes and bewitched his heart. But the king would not listen to this; he ordered the music to sound, the daintiest dishes to be served, and the loveliest maidens to dance.

Aftewards he led her through fragrant gardens and lofty halls, but not a smile appeared on her lips or sparkled in her eyes. She looked the very picture of grief. Then the king opened the door of a little chamber in which she was to sleep; it was adorned with rich green tapestry, and resembled the cave in which he had found her. On the floor lay the bundle of flax which she had spun from the nettles, and under the ceiling hung the coat she had made. These things had been brought away from the cave as curiosities by one of the huntsmen.

"Here you can dream yourself back again in the old home in the cave," said the king; "here is the work with which you employed yourself. It will amuse you now in the midst of all this splendor to think of that time."

When Eliza saw all these things which lay so near her heart, a smile played around her mouth, and the crimson blood rushed to her cheeks.

She thought of her brothers, and their release made her so joyful that she kissed the king's hand. Then he pressed her to his heart.

Very soon the joyous church bells announced the marriage feast, and that the beautiful dumb girl out of the wood was to be made the queen of the country. Then the archbishop whispered wicked words in the king's ear, but they did not sink into his heart. The marriage was still to take place, and the archbishop himself had to place the crown on the bride's head; in his wicked spite, he pressed the narrow circlet so tightly on her forehead that it caused her pain. But a heavier weight encircled her heart—sorrow for her brothers. She felt not bodily pain. Her mouth was closed; a single word would cost the lives of her brothers. But she loved the kind, handsome king, who did everything to make her happy more and more each day; she loved him with all her heart, and her eyes beamed with the love she dared not speak. Oh! If she had only been able to confide in him and tell him of her grief. But dumb she must remain till her task was finished.

Therefore at night she crept away into her little chamber, which had been decked out to look like the cave, and quickly wove one coat after another. But when she began the seventh she found she had no more flax. She knew that the nettles she wanted to use grew in the churchyard, and that she must pluck them herself. How should she get out there?

"Oh, what is the pain in my fingers to the torment which my heart endures?" said she. "I must venture to the churchyard; I shall not be denied help from heaven."

Then with a trembling heart, as if she were about to perform a wicked deed, she crept into the garden in the broad moonlight, and passed through the narrow walks and the deserted streets, till she reached the churchyard. Then she saw on one of the broad tombstones a group of ghouls. These hideous creatures took off their rags, as if they intended to bathe, and then clawing open the fresh graves with their long, skinny fingers, pulled out the dead bodies and ate the flesh! Eliza had to pass close by them, and they fixed their wicked glances upon her, but she prayed silently, gathered the burning nettles, and carried them home with her to the castle.

One person only had seen her, and that was the archbishop—he was awake while everybody was asleep. Now he thought his opinion was evidently correct. All was not right with the queen. She was a witch, and had bewitched the king and all the people. Secretly he told the king what he had seen and what he feared, and as the hard words came from his tongue, the carved images of the saints shook their heads as if they would say, "It is not so. Eliza is innocent."

But the archbishop interpreted it in another way; he believed that they witnessed against her, and were shaking their heads at her wickedness. Two large tears rolled down the king's cheeks, and he went home with doubt in his heart, and at night he pretended to sleep, but there came no real sleep to his eyes, for he saw Eliza get up every night and disappear in her own chamber. From day to day his brow became darker, and Eliza saw it and did not understand the reason, but it alarmed her and made her heart tremble for her brothers. Her hot tears glittered like pearls on the regal velvet and diamonds, while all who saw her were wishing they could be queens.

In the meantime she had almost finished her task; only one coat of mail was wanting, but she had no flax left, and not a single nettle. Once more only, and for the last time, must she venture to the churchyard and pluck a few handfuls. She thought with terror of the solitary walk, and of the horrible ghouls, but her will was firm, as well as her trust in Providence. Eliza went, and the king and the archbishop followed her. They saw her vanish through the wicket gate into the churchyard, and when they came nearer they saw the ghouls sitting on the tombstone, as Eliza had seen them, and the king turned away his head, for he thought she was with them—she whose head had rested on his breast that very evening.

"The people must condemn her," said he, and she was very quickly condemned by everyone to suffer death by fire. Away from the gorgeous regal halls was she led to a dark, dreary cell, where the wind whistled through the iron bars. Instead of the velvet and silk dresses, they gave her the coats of mail which she had woven to cover her, and the bundle of nettles for a pillow; but nothing they could give her would have pleased her more. She continued her task with joy, and prayed for help, while the street boys sang jeering songs about her, and not a soul comforted her with a kind word.

Towards evening, she heard at the grating the flutter of a swan's wing; it was her youngest brother—he had found his sister, and she sobbed for joy, although she knew that very likely this would be the last night she would have to live. But still she could hope, for her task was almost finished, and her brothers were come. Then the archbishop arrived, to be with her during her last hours, as he had promised the king. But she shook her head and begged him, by looks and gestures, not to stay; for in this night she knew she must finish her task, otherwise all her pain and tears and sleepless nights would have been suffered in vain. The archbishop withdrew, uttering bitter words against her; but poor Eliza knew that she was innocent, and diligently continued her work.

The little mice ran about the floor, they dragged the nettles to her feet, to help as well as they could; and the thrush sat outside the grating of the window, and sang to her the whole night long, as sweetly as possible, to keep up her spirits.

It was still twilight, and at least an hour before sunrise, when the eleven brothers stood at the castle gate and demanded to be brought before the king. They were told it could not be, it was yet almost night, and as the king slept they dared not disturb him. They threatened, they entreated. Then the guard appeared, and even the king himself, inquiring what all the noise meant. At this moment the sun rose. The eleven brothers were seen no more, but eleven wild swans flew away over the castle.

And now all the people came streaming forth from the gates of the city, to see the witch burned. An old horse drew the cart on which she sat. They had dressed her in a garment of coarse sackcloth. Her lovely hair hung loose on her shoulders, her cheeks were deadly pale, her lips moved silently, while her fingers still worked at the green flax. Even on the way to death, she would not give up her task. The ten coats of mail lay at her feet, she was working hard at the eleventh, while the mob jeered her and said, "See the witch, how she mutters! She has no hymn book in her hand. She sits there with her ugly sorcery. Let us tear it in a thousand pieces."

And then they pressed towards her, and would have destroyed the coats of mail, but at the same moment eleven wild swans flew over her and alighted on the cart. Then they flapped their large wings, and the crowd drew on one side in alarm.

"It is a sign from heaven that she is innocent," whispered many of them; but they ventured not to say it aloud.

As the executioner seized her by the hand to lift her out of the cart, she hastily threw the eleven coats of mail over the swans, and they immediately became eleven handsome princes; but the youngest had a swan's wing instead of an arm; for she had not been able to finish the last sleeve of the coat.

"Now I may speak," she exclaimed. "I am innocent."

Then the people, who saw what happened, bowed to her as before a saint; but she sank lifeless in her brothers' arms, overcome with suspense, anguish, and pain.

"Yes, she is innocent," said the eldest brother; and then he related all that had taken place; and while he spoke there rose in the air a fragrance as from millions of roses. Every piece of faggot in the pile had taken root, and threw out branches, and appeared a thick hedge, large and high, covered with roses; while above all bloomed a white and shining flower, that glittered like a star. This flower the king plucked, and placed in Eliza's bosom, when she awoke from her swoon, with peace and happiness in her heart. And all the church bells rang of themselves, and the birds came in great troops. And a marriage procession returned to the castle, such as no king had ever before seen.

# THE LITTLE MERMAID

F ar out in the ocean, where the water is as blue as the prettiest
cornflower, and as clear as crystal, it is very, very deep; so deep,
indeed, that no cable could fathom it: many church steeples,
piled one upon another, would not reach from the ground beneath
to the surface of the water above. There dwell the Sea King and his
subjects. We must not imagine that there is nothing at the bottom of
the sea but bare yellow sand. No, indeed; the most singular flowers and
plants grow there; the leaves and stems of which are so pliant, that the
slightest agitation of the water causes them to stir as if they had life.
Fishes, both large and small, glide between the branches, as birds fly
among the trees here upon land. In the deepest spot of all stands the
castle of the Sea King. Its walls are built of coral, and the long, gothic
windows are of the clearest amber. The roof is formed of shells that

open and close as the water flows over them. Their appearance is very beautiful, for in each lies a glittering pearl, which would be fit for the diadem of a queen.

The Sea King had been a widower for many years, and his aged mother kept house for him. She was a very wise woman, and exceedingly proud of her high birth; on that account she wore twelve oysters on her tail; while others, also of high rank, were only allowed to wear six. She was, however, deserving of very great praise, especially for her care of the little sea princesses, her granddaughters. They were six beautiful children, but the youngest was the prettiest of them all; her skin was as clear and delicate as a rose leaf, and her eyes as blue as the deepest sea; but, like all the others, she had no feet, and her body ended in a fish's tail.

All day long they played in the great halls of the castle, or among the living flowers that grew out of the walls. The large amber windows were open, and the fish swam in, just as the swallows fly into our houses when we open the windows, excepting that the fishes swam up to the princesses, ate out of their hands, and allowed themselves to be stroked. Outside the castle there was a beautiful garden, in which grew bright red and dark blue flowers, and blossoms like flames of fire; the fruit glittered like gold, and the leaves and stems waved to and fro continually. The earth itself was the finest sand, but blue as the flame of burning sulfur. Over everything lay a peculiar blue radiance, as if it were surrounded by the air from above, through which the blue sky shone, instead of the dark depths of the sea. In calm weather the sun could be seen, looking like a purple flower, with the light streaming from its cup.

*She cared for nothing but her pretty red flowers, except for a beautiful marble statue.*

Each of the young princesses had a little plot of ground in the garden, where she might dig and plant as she pleased. One arranged her flower bed into the form of a whale; another thought it better to make hers like the figure of a little mermaid; but that of the youngest was round like the sun, and contained flowers as red as his rays at sunset. She was a strange child, quiet and thoughtful; and while her sisters would be delighted with the wonderful things which they obtained from the wrecks of vessels, she cared for nothing but her pretty red flowers, like the sun, except for a beautiful marble statue. It was the representation of a handsome boy, carved out of pure white stone, which had fallen to the bottom of the sea from a wreck. She planted by the statue a rose-colored weeping willow. It grew splendidly, and very soon hung its fresh branches over the statue, almost down to the blue sands. The shadow had a violet tint, and waved to and fro like the branches; it seemed as if the crown of the tree and the root were at play, and trying to kiss each other. Nothing gave her so much pleasure as to hear about the world above the sea. She made her old grandmother tell her all she knew of the ships and of the towns, the people and the animals. To her it seemed most wonderful and beautiful to hear that the flowers of the land should have fragrance, and not those below the sea; that the trees of the forest should be green; and that the fishes among the trees could sing so sweetly, that it was quite a pleasure to hear them. Her grandmother called the little birds fishes, or she would not have understood her; for she had never seen birds.

"When you have reached your fifteenth year," said the grandmother, "you will have permission to rise up out of the sea, to sit on the rocks in the moonlight, while the great ships are sailing by; and then you will see both forests and towns."

In the following year, one of the sisters would be fifteen: but as each was a year younger than the other, the youngest would have to wait five years before her turn came to rise up from the bottom of the ocean, and see the earth as we do. However, each promised to tell the others what she saw on her first visit, and what she thought the most beautiful; for their grandmother could not tell them enough; there were so many things on which they wanted information. None of them longed so much for her turn to come as the youngest, she who had the longest time to wait, and who was so quiet and thoughtful. Many nights she stood by the open window, looking up through the dark blue water, and watching the fish as they splashed about with their fins and tails. She could see the moon and stars shining faintly; but through the water they looked larger than they do to our eyes. When something like a black cloud passed between her and them, she knew that it was either a whale swimming over her head, or a ship full of human beings, who never imagined that a pretty little mermaid was standing beneath them, holding out her white hands towards the keel of their ship.

As soon as the eldest was fifteen, she was allowed to rise to the surface of the ocean. When she came back, she had hundreds of things to talk about; but the most beautiful, she said, was to lie in the moonlight, on a sandbank, in the quiet sea, near the coast, and to gaze on a large town nearby, where the lights were twinkling like hundreds of stars; to listen to the sounds of the music, the noise of carriages, and the voices of human beings, and then to hear the merry bells peal out from the church steeples; and because she could not go near to all those wonderful things, she longed for them more than ever. Oh, did not the youngest sister listen eagerly to all these descriptions? And afterwards, when she stood at the open window looking up through the dark blue water, she thought of the great city, with all its bustle and noise, and even fancied she could hear the sound of the church bells, down in the depths of the sea.

In another year the second sister received permission to rise to the surface of the water, and to swim about where she pleased. She rose just as the sun was setting, and this, she said, was the most beautiful sight of all. The whole sky looked like gold, while violet and rose-colored clouds, which she could not describe, floated over her; and, still more rapidly than the clouds, flew a large flock of wild swans towards the setting sun, looking like a long white veil across the sea. She also swam towards the sun; but it sunk into the waves, and the rosy tints faded from the clouds and from the sea.

The third sister's turn followed; she was the boldest of them all, and she swam up a broad river that emptied itself into the sea. On the banks she saw green hills covered with beautiful vines; palaces and castles peeped out from amid the proud trees of the forest; she heard the birds singing, and the rays of the sun were so powerful that she was obliged often to dive down under the water to cool her burning face. In a narrow creek she found a whole troop of little human children, quite naked, and sporting about in the water; she wanted to play with them, but they fled in a great fright; and then a little black animal came to the water; it was a dog, but she did not know that, for she had never before seen one. This animal barked at her so terribly that she became frightened, and rushed back to the open sea. But she said she should never forget the beautiful forest, the green hills, and the pretty little children who could swim in the water, although they had not fish's tails.

The fourth sister was more timid; she remained in the midst of the sea, but she said it was quite as beautiful there as nearer the land. She could see for so many miles around her, and the sky above looked like a bell of glass. She had seen the ships, but at such a great distance that they looked like seagulls. The dolphins sported in the waves, and the great whales spouted water from their nostrils till it seemed as if a hundred fountains were playing in every direction.

The fifth sister's birthday occurred in the winter; so when her turn

*In a narrow creek she found a whole troop of little human children.*

came, she saw what the others had not seen the first time they went up. The sea looked quite green, and large icebergs were floating about, each like a pearl, she said, but larger and loftier than the churches built by men. They were of the most singular shapes, and glittered like diamonds. She had seated herself upon one of the largest, and let the wind play with her long hair, and she remarked that all the ships sailed by rapidly, and steered as far away as they could from the iceberg, as if they were afraid of it. Towards evening, as the sun went down, dark clouds covered the sky, the thunder rolled and the lightning flashed, and the red light glowed on the icebergs as they rocked and tossed on the heaving sea. On all the ships the sails were reefed with fear and trembling, while she sat calmly on the floating iceberg, watching the blue lightning, as it darted its forked flashes into the sea.

When first the sisters had permission to rise to the surface, they were each delighted with the new and beautiful sights they saw; but now, as grown-up girls, they could go when they pleased, and they had become indifferent about it. They wished themselves back again in the water, and after a month had passed they said it was much more beautiful down below, and pleasanter to be at home. Yet often, in the evening hours, the five sisters would twine their arms around each other and rise to the surface in a row. They had more beautiful voices than any human being could have; and before the approach of a storm, and when they expected a ship would be lost, they swam before the vessel and sang sweetly of the delights to be found in the depths of the sea, and begging the sailors not to fear if they sank to the bottom. But the sailors could not understand the song, they took it for the howling of the storm. And these things were never to be beautiful for them; for if the ship sank, the men were drowned, and their dead bodies alone reached the palace of the Sea King.

When the sisters rose, arm-in-arm, through the water in this way, their youngest sister would stand quite alone, looking after them, ready to cry, only that the mermaids have no tears, and therefore they suffer more. "Oh, were I but fifteen years old," said she. "I know that I shall love the world up there, and all the people who live in it."

At last she reached her fifteenth year. "Well, now, you are grown up," said the old dowager, her grandmother; "so you must let me adorn you like your other sisters"; and she placed a wreath of white lilies in her hair, and every flower leaf was half a pearl. Then the old lady ordered eight great oysters to attach themselves to the tail of the princess to show her high rank.

"But they hurt me so," said the little mermaid.

"Pride must suffer pain," replied the old lady. Oh, how gladly she would have shaken off all this grandeur, and laid aside the heavy wreath! The red flowers in her own garden would have suited her much better, but she could not help herself: so she said, "Farewell," and rose as lightly as a bubble to the surface of the water. The sun had just set as she raised her head above the waves; but the clouds were tinted with crimson and gold, and through the glimmering twilight beamed the evening star in all its beauty. The sea was calm, and the air mild and fresh. A large ship with three masts lay becalmed on the water, with only one sail set; for not a breeze stiffed, and the sailors sat idle on deck or among the rigging. There was music and song on board; and, as darkness came on, a hundred colored lanterns were lighted, as if the flags of all nations waved in the air. The little mermaid swam close to the cabin windows; and now and then, as the waves lifted her up, she could look in through clear glass windowpanes and see a number of well-dressed people within. Among them was a young prince, the most beautiful of all, with large black eyes; he was sixteen years of age, and his birthday was being kept with much rejoicing. The sailors were dancing on deck, but when the prince came out of the cabin, more than a hundred rockets rose in the air, making it as bright as day. The little mermaid was so startled that she dived under water; and when she again stretched out her head, it appeared as if all the stars of heaven were falling around her, she had never seen such fireworks before. Great suns spurted fire about, splendid fireflies flew into the blue air, and everything was reflected in the clear, calm sea beneath. The ship itself was so brightly illuminated that all the people, and even the smallest rope, could be distinctly and plainly seen. And how handsome the young prince looked, as he pressed the hands of all present and smiled at them, while the music resounded through the clear night air.

It was very late; yet the little mermaid could not take her eyes from the ship, or from the beautiful prince. The colored lanterns had been extinguished, no more rockets rose in the air, and the cannon had ceased firing; but the sea became restless, and a moaning, grumbling sound could be heard beneath the waves: still the little mermaid remained by the cabin window, rocking up and down on the water, which enabled her to look in. After a while, the sails were quickly unfurled, and the noble ship continued her passage; but soon the waves rose higher, heavy clouds darkened the sky, and lightning appeared in the distance.

A dreadful storm was approaching; once more the sails were reefed, and the great ship pursued her flying course over the raging sea. The waves rose mountains high, as if they would have overtopped the mast; but the ship dived like a swan between them, and then rose again on their lofty, foaming crests. To the little mermaid this appeared pleasant sport; not so to the sailors. At length the ship groaned and creaked, the thick planks gave way under the lashing of the sea as it broke over the deck, the mainmast snapped asunder like a reed, the ship lay over on her side, and the water rushed in.

The little mermaid now perceived that the crew were in danger; even she herself was obliged to be careful to avoid the beams and planks of the wreck which lay scattered on the water. At one moment it was so pitch dark that she could not see a single object, but a flash of lightning revealed the whole scene; she could see everyone who had been on board excepting the prince; when the ship parted, she had seen him sink into the deep waves, and she was glad, for she thought he would now be with her; and then she remembered that human beings could not live in the water, so that when he got down to her father's palace he would be quite dead. But he must not die. So she swam about among the beams and planks strewn across the surface of the sea, forgetting that they could crush her to pieces. Then she dived deeply under the dark waters, rising and falling with the waves, till at length she managed to reach the young prince, who was fast losing the power of swimming in that stormy sea. His limbs were failing him, his beautiful eyes were closed, and he would have died had not the little mermaid come to his assistance. She held his head above the water, and let the waves drift them where they would.

In the morning the storm had ceased; but of the ship not a single fragment could be seen. The sun rose up red and glowing from the water, and its beams brought back the hue of health to the prince's cheeks; but his eyes remained closed. The mermaid kissed his high, smooth forehead, and stroked back his wet hair; he seemed to her like the marble statue in her little garden, and she kissed him again, and wished that he might live.

Presently they came in sight of land; she saw lofty blue mountains, on which the white snow rested as if a flock of swans were lying upon them. Near the coast were beautiful green forests, and close by stood a large building, whether a church or a convent she could not tell. Orange and citron trees grew in the garden, and before the door stood lofty palms. The sea here formed a little bay, in which the water was quite still, but very deep; so she swam with the handsome prince to the beach, which was covered with fine, white sand, and there she laid him in the warm sunshine, taking care to raise his head higher than his body. Then bells sounded in the large white building, and a number of young girls came into the garden. The little mermaid swam out farther from the shore and placed herself between some high rocks that rose out of the water; then she covered her head and neck with the foam of the sea so that her little face might not be seen, and watched to see what would become of the poor prince. She did not wait long before she saw a young girl approach the spot where he lay. She seemed frightened at first, but only for a moment; then she fetched a number of people, and the mermaid saw that the prince came to life again, and smiled upon those who stood around him. But to her he sent no smile; he knew not that she had saved him. This made her very unhappy, and when he was led away into the great building, she dived down sorrowfully into the water and returned to her father's castle.

She had always been silent and thoughtful, and now she was more so than ever. Her sisters asked her what she had seen during her first visit to the surface of the water; but she would tell them nothing. Many an evening and morning did she rise to the place where she had left the prince. She saw the fruits in the garden ripen till they were gathered, the snow on the tops of the mountains melt away; but she never saw the prince, and therefore she returned home, always more sorrowful than before. It was her only comfort to sit in her own little garden and fling her arm around the beautiful marble statue which was like the prince; but she gave up tending her flowers, and they grew in wild confusion over the paths, twining their long leaves and stems around the branches of the trees, so that the whole place became dark and gloomy. At length she could bear it no longer, and told one of her sisters all about it. Then the others heard the secret, and very soon it became known to two mermaids whose intimate friend happened to know who the prince was. She had also seen the festival on board the ship, and she told them where the prince came from, and where his palace stood.

"Come, little sister," said the other princesses; then they entwined their arms and rose up in a long row to the surface of the water, close by the spot where they knew the prince's palace stood. It was built of bright yellow shining stone, with long flights of marble steps, one of which reached down to the sea. Splendid gilded cupolas rose over the roof, and between the pillars that surrounded the whole building stood lifelike statues of marble. Through the clear crystal of the lofty windows could be seen noble rooms with costly silk curtains and hangings of tapestry, while the walls were covered with beautiful paintings which were a pleasure to look at. In the center of the largest saloon a fountain threw its sparkling jets high up into the glass cupola of the ceiling, through which the sun shone down upon the water and upon the beautiful plants growing around the basin of the fountain. Now that she knew where he lived, she spent many an evening and many a night on the water near the palace. She would swim much nearer the shore than any of the others ventured to do; indeed once she went up the narrow channel under the marble balcony, which threw a

broad shadow on the water. Here she would sit and watch the young prince, who thought himself quite alone in the bright moonlight. She saw him many times of an evening sailing in a pleasant boat, with music playing and flags waving. She peeped out from among the green rushes, and if the wind caught her long silvery-white veil, those who saw it believed it to be a swan spreading out its wings. On many a night, too, when the fishermen, with their torches, were out at sea, she heard them relate so many good things about the doings of the young prince, that she was glad she had saved his life when he had been tossed about half-dead on the waves. And she remembered that his head had rested on her bosom, and how heartily she had kissed him; but he knew nothing of all this, and could not even dream of her. She grew more and more fond of human beings, and wished more and more to be able to wander about with those whose world seemed to be so much larger than her own. They could fly over the sea in ships, and mount the high hills which were far above the clouds; and the lands they possessed, their woods and their fields, stretched far away beyond the reach of her sight. There was so much that she wished to know, and her sisters were unable to answer all her questions. Then she approached her old grandmother, who knew all about the upper world, which she very rightly called the lands above the sea.

"If human beings are not drowned," asked the little mermaid, "can they live forever? Do they never die as we do here in the sea?"

"Yes," replied the old lady, "they must also die, and their term of life is even shorter than ours. We sometimes live to three hundred years, but when we cease to exist here we only become the foam on the surface of the water, and we have not even a grave down here of those we love. We have not immortal souls, we shall never live again; but, like the green seaweed, when once it has been cut off, we can never flourish more. Human beings, on the contrary, have a soul which lives forever, lives after the body has been turned to dust. It rises up through the clear, pure air beyond the glittering stars. As we rise out of the water, and behold all the land of the earth, so do they rise to unknown and glorious regions which we shall never see."

"Why have not we an immortal soul?" asked the little mermaid mournfully. "I would give gladly all the hundreds of years that I have to live, to be a human being only for one day, and to have the hope of knowing the happiness of that glorious world above the stars."

"You must not think of that," said the old woman; "we feel ourselves to be much happier and much better off than human beings."

"So I shall die," said the little mermaid, "and as the foam of the sea I shall be driven about never again to hear the music of the waves, or to see the pretty flowers nor the red sun. Is there anything I can do to win an immortal soul?"

"No," said the old woman, "unless a man were to love you so much that you were more to him than his father or mother; and if all his thoughts and all his love were fixed upon you, and the priest placed his right hand in yours, and he promised to be true to you here and hereafter, then his soul would glide into your body and you would obtain a share in the future happiness of mankind. He would give a soul to you and retain his own as well; but this can never happen. Your fish's tail, which among us is considered so beautiful, is thought on earth to be quite ugly; they do not know any better, and they think it necessary to have two stout props, which they call legs, in order to be handsome."

Then the little mermaid sighed, and looked sorrowfully at her fish's tail. "Let us be happy," said the old lady, "and dart and spring about during the three hundred years that we have to live, which is really quite long enough; after that we can rest ourselves all the better. This evening we are going to have a court ball."

It is one of those splendid sights which we can never see on earth. The walls and the ceiling of the large ballroom were of thick but transparent crystal. Many hundreds of colossal shells, some of a deep red, others of a grass green, stood on each side in rows, with blue fire in them, which lighted up the whole saloon and shone through the walls, so that the sea was also illuminated. Innumerable fishes, great and small, swam past the crystal walls; on some of them the scales glowed with a purple brilliancy, and on others they shone like silver and gold. Through the halls flowed a broad stream, and in it danced the mermen and the mermaids to the music of their own sweet singing. No one on earth has such a lovely voice as theirs. The little mermaid sang more sweetly than them all. The whole court applauded her with hands and tails; and for a moment her heart felt quite gay, for she knew she had the loveliest voice of any on earth or in the sea.

But she soon thought again of the world above her, for she could not forget the charming prince, nor her sorrow that she had not an immortal soul like his; therefore she crept away silently out of her father's palace, and while everything within was gladness and song, she sat in her own little garden sorrowful and alone. Then she heard the bugle sounding through the water, and thought, "He is certainly sailing above, he on whom my wishes depend, and in whose hands I should like to place the happiness of my life. I will risk everything for him, and to win an immortal soul, while my sisters are dancing in my father's palace, I will go to the sea witch, of whom I have always been so much afraid, but she can give me counsel and help."

And then the little mermaid went out from her garden, and took the road to the foaming whirlpools, behind which the sorceress lived. She had never been that way before: neither flowers nor grass grew there; nothing but bare, gray, sandy ground stretched out to the whirlpool, where the water, like foaming mill wheels, whirled around everything that it seized, and cast it into the fathomless deep. Through the midst of these crushing whirlpools the little mermaid was obliged to pass, to reach the dominions of the sea witch; and also for a long distance the only road lay right across a quantity of warm, bubbling mire, called by the witch her turfmoor. Beyond this stood her house, in the center of a strange forest, in which all the trees and flowers were polypi, half animals and half plants; they looked like serpents with a hundred heads growing out of the ground. The branches were long slimy arms, with fingers like flexible worms, moving limb after limb from the root to the top. All that could be reached in the sea they seized upon and held fast, so that it never escaped from their clutches.

The little mermaid was so alarmed at what she saw that she stood still, and her heart beat with fear, and she was very nearly turning back; but she thought of the prince, and of the human soul for which she longed, and her courage returned. She fastened her long flowing hair around her head, so that the polypi might not seize hold of it. She laid her hands together across her bosom, and then she darted forward as a fish shoots through the water, between the supple arms and fingers of the ugly polypi, which were stretched out on each side of her. She saw that each held in its grasp something it had seized with its numerous little arms, as if they were iron bands. The white skeletons of human beings who had perished at sea, and had sunk down into the deep waters, skeletons of land animals, oars, rudders, and chests of ships were lying tightly grasped by their clinging arms; even a little mermaid, whom they had caught and strangled; and this seemed the most shocking of all to the little princess.

She now came to a space of marshy ground in the wood where large, fat water snakes were rolling in the mire and showing their ugly, drab-colored bodies. In the midst of this spot stood a house, built with the bones of shipwrecked human beings. There sat the sea witch, allowing a toad to eat from her mouth, just as people sometimes feed a canary with a piece of sugar. She called the ugly water snakes her little chickens, and allowed them to crawl all over her bosom.

"I know what you want," said the sea witch; "it is very stupid of you, but you shall have your way, and it will bring you to sorrow, my pretty princess. You want to get rid of your fish's tail, and to have two supports instead of it, like human beings on earth, so that the young prince may fall in love with you, and that you may have an immortal soul." And then the witch laughed so loud and disgustingly that the toad and the snakes fell to the ground, and lay there wriggling about.

"You are but just in time," said the witch; "for after sunrise tomorrow I should not be able to help you till the end of another year. I will prepare a draft for you, with which you must swim to land tomorrow before sunrise, and sit down on the shore and drink it. Your tail will then disappear, and shrink up into what mankind calls legs, and you will feel great pain, as if a sword were passing through you. But all who see you will say that you are the prettiest little human being they ever saw. You will still have the same floating gracefulness of movement, and no dancer will ever tread so lightly; but at every step you take it will feel as if you were treading upon sharp knives, and that the blood must flow. If you will bear all this, I will help you."

"Yes, I will," said the little princess in a trembling voice, as she thought of the prince and the immortal soul.

"But think again," said the witch; "for when once your shape has become like a human being, you can no more be a mermaid. You will never return through the water to your sisters, or to your father's palace again; and if you do not win the love of the prince, so that he is willing to forget his father and mother for your sake, and to love you with his whole soul, and allow the priest to join your hands that you may be man and wife, then you will never have an immortal soul. The first morning after he marries another, your heart will break and you will become foam on the crest of the waves."

"I will do it," said the little mermaid, and she became pale as death.

"But I must be paid also," said the witch, "and it is not a trifle that I ask. You have the sweetest voice of any who dwell here in the depths of the sea, and you believe that you will be able to charm the prince with it also, but this voice you must give to me; the best thing you possess will I have for the price of my draft. My own blood must be mixed with it, that it may be as sharp as a two-edged sword."

"But if you take away my voice," said the little mermaid, "what is left for me?"

"Your beautiful form, your graceful walk, and your expressive eyes; surely with these you can enchain a man's heart. Well, have you lost your courage? Put out your little tongue that I may cut it off as my payment; then you shall have the powerful draft."

"It shall be," said the little mermaid.

Then the witch placed her cauldron on the fire, to prepare the magic draft.

"Cleanliness is a good thing," said she, scouring the vessel with snakes, which she had tied together in a large knot; then she pricked herself in the breast, and let the black blood drop into it. The steam that rose formed itself into such horrible shapes that no one could look at them without fear. Every moment the witch threw something else into the vessel, and when it began to boil, the sound was like the weeping of a crocodile. When at last the magic draft was ready, it looked like the clearest water. "There it is for you," said the witch. Then she cut off the mermaid's tongue, so that she became dumb and would never again speak or sing. "If the polypi should seize hold of you as you return through the wood," said the witch, "throw over them a few drops of the potion, and their fingers will be torn into a thousand pieces." But the little mermaid had no occasion to do this, for the polypi sprang back in terror when they caught sight of the glittering draft, which shone in her hand like a twinkling star.

W HEATH ROBINSON

So she passed quickly through the wood and the marsh, and between the rushing whirlpools. She saw that in her father's palace the torches in the ballroom were extinguished, and all within asleep; but she did not venture to go in to them, for now she was dumb and going to leave them forever, she felt as if her heart would break. She stole into the garden, took a flower from the flower beds of each of her sisters, kissed her hand a thousand times towards the palace, and then rose up through the dark blue waters. The sun had not risen when she came in sight of the prince's palace, and approached the beautiful marble steps, but the moon shone clear and bright. Then the little mermaid drank the magic draft, and it seemed as if a two-edged sword went through her delicate body: she fell into a swoon, and lay like one dead.

When the sun arose and shone over the sea, she recovered and felt a sharp pain; but just before her stood the handsome young prince. He fixed his coal-black eyes upon her so earnestly that she cast down her own, and then became aware that her fish's tail was gone, and that she had as pretty a pair of white legs and tiny feet as any little maiden could have; but she had no clothes, so she wrapped herself in her long, thick hair. The prince asked her who she was and where she came from, and she looked at him mildly and sorrowfully with her deep blue eyes; but she could not speak.

Every step she took was as the witch had said it would be; she felt as if treading upon the points of needles or sharp knives, but she bore it willingly, and stepped as lightly by the prince's side as a soap bubble, so that he and all who saw her wondered at her graceful swaying movements. She was very soon arrayed in costly robes of silk and muslin, and was the most beautiful creature in the palace; but she was dumb, and could neither speak nor sing.

Beautiful female slaves, dressed in silk and gold, stepped forward and sang before the prince and his royal parents: one sang better than all the others, and the prince clapped his hands and smiled at her. This was great sorrow to the little mermaid; she knew how much more sweetly she herself could sing once, and she thought, "Oh, if he could only know that I have given away my voice forever, to be with him!"

The slaves next performed some pretty fairylike dances to the sound of beautiful music. Then the little mermaid raised her lovely white arms, stood on the tips of her toes, and glided over the floor, and danced as no one yet had been able to dance. At each moment her beauty became more revealed, and her expressive eyes appealed more directly to the heart than the songs of the slaves. Everyone was enchanted, especially the prince, who called her his little foundling; and she danced again quite readily to please him, though each time her foot touched the floor it seemed as if she trod on sharp knives.

The prince said she should remain with him always, and she received permission to sleep at his door, on a velvet cushion. He had a page's dress made for her, that she might accompany him on horseback. They rode together through the sweet-scented woods, where the green boughs touched their shoulders, and the little birds sang among the fresh leaves. She climbed with the prince to the tops of high mountains; and although her tender feet bled so that even her steps were marked, she only laughed, and followed him till they could see the clouds beneath them looking like a flock of birds traveling to distant lands. While at the prince's palace, and when all the household were asleep, she would go and sit on the broad marble steps; for it eased her burning feet to bathe them in the cold seawater; and then she thought of all those below in the deep.

Once during the night her sisters came up arm-in-arm, singing sorrowfully, as they floated on the water. She beckoned to them, and then they recognized her, and told her how she had grieved them. After that, they came to the same place every night; and once she saw in the distance her old grandmother, who had not been to the surface of the sea for many years, and the old Sea King, her father, with his crown on his head. They stretched out their hands towards her, but they did not venture so near the land as her sisters did.

As the days passed, she loved the prince more fondly, and he loved her as he would love a little child, but it never came into his head to make her his wife; yet, unless he married her, she could not receive an immortal soul; and, on the morning after his marriage with another, she would dissolve into the foam of the sea.

"Do you not love me the best of them all?" the eyes of the little mermaid seemed to say, when he took her in his arms, and kissed her fair forehead.

"Yes, you are dear to me," said the prince; "for you have the best heart, and you are the most devoted to me; you are like a young maiden whom I once saw, but whom I shall never meet again. I was in a ship that was wrecked, and the waves cast me ashore near a holy temple, where several young maidens performed the service. The youngest of them found me on the shore, and saved my life. I saw her but twice, and she is the only one in the world whom I could love; but you are like her, and you have almost driven her image out of my mind. She belongs to the holy temple, and my good fortune has sent you to me instead of her; and we will never part."

"Ah, he knows not that it was I who saved his life," thought the little mermaid. "I carried him over the sea to the wood where the temple stands: I sat beneath the foam, and watched till the human beings came to help him. I saw the pretty maiden that he loves better than he loves me"; and the mermaid sighed deeply, but she could not shed tears. "He says the maiden belongs to the holy temple, therefore she will never return to the world. They will meet no more: while I am by his side, and see him every day. I will take care of him, and love him, and give up my life for his sake."

Very soon it was said that the prince must marry, and that the beautiful daughter of a neighboring king would be his wife, for a fine ship was being fitted out. Although the prince gave out that he merely intended to pay a visit to the king, it was generally supposed that he really went to see his daughter. A great company were to go with him.

The little mermaid smiled and shook her head. She knew the prince's thoughts better than any of the others.

"I must travel," he had said to her; "I must see this beautiful princess; my parents desire it; but they will not oblige me to bring her home as my bride. I cannot love her; she is not like the beautiful maiden in the temple, whom you resemble. If I were forced to choose a bride, I would rather choose you, my dumb foundling, with those expressive eyes." And then he kissed her rosy mouth, played with her long waving hair, and laid his head on her heart, while she dreamed of human happiness and an immortal soul.

"You are not afraid of the sea, my dumb child," said he, as they stood on the deck of the noble ship which was to carry them to the country of the neighboring king. And then he told her of storm and of calm, of strange fishes in the deep beneath them, and of what the divers had seen there; and she smiled at his descriptions, for she knew better than anyone what wonders were at the bottom of the sea.

In the moonlight, when all on board were asleep, excepting the man at the helm, who was steering, she sat on the deck, gazing down through the clear water. She thought she could distinguish her father's castle, and upon it her aged grandmother, with the silver crown on her head, looking through the rushing tide at the keel of the vessel. Then her sisters came up on the waves, and gazed at her mournfully, wringing their white hands. She beckoned to them and smiled, and wanted to tell them how happy and well off she was; but the cabin boy approached, and when her sisters dived down he thought it was only the foam of the sea which he saw.

The next morning the ship sailed into the harbor of a beautiful town belonging to the king whom the prince was going to visit. The church bells were ringing, and from the high towers sounded a flourish of trumpets; and soldiers, with flying colors and glittering bayonets, lined the rocks through which they passed. Every day was a festival; balls and entertainments followed one another.

But the princess had not yet appeared. People said that she was being brought up and educated in a religious house, where she was learning every royal virtue. At last she came. Then the little mermaid, who was very anxious to see whether she was really beautiful, was obliged to acknowledge that she had never seen a more perfect vision of beauty. Her skin was delicately fair, and beneath her long dark eyelashes her laughing blue eyes shone with truth and purity.

"It was you," said the prince, "who saved my life when I lay dead on the beach," and he folded his blushing bride in his arms. "Oh, I am too happy," said he to the little mermaid; "my fondest hopes are all fulfilled. You will rejoice at my happiness; for your devotion to me is great and sincere."

The little mermaid kissed his hand, and felt as if her heart were already broken. His wedding morning would bring death to her, and she would change into the foam of the sea. All the church bells rung, and the heralds rode about the town proclaiming the betrothal. Perfumed oil was burning in costly silver lamps on every altar. The priests waved the censers, while the bride and bridegroom joined their hands and received the blessing of the bishop. The little mermaid, dressed in silk and gold, held up the bride's train; but her ears heard nothing of the festive music, and her eyes saw not the holy ceremony; she thought of the night of death which was coming to her, and of all she had lost in the world.

On the same evening the bride and bridegroom went on board the ship; cannons were roaring, flags waving, and in the center of the ship a costly tent of purple and gold had been erected. It contained elegant couches, for the reception of the bridal pair during the night. The ship, with swelling sails and a favorable wind, glided away smoothly and lightly over the calm sea. When it grew dark a number of colored lamps were lit, and the sailors danced merrily on the deck. The little mermaid could not help thinking of her first rising out of the sea, when she had seen similar festivities and joys; and she joined in the dance, poised herself in the air as a swallow when he pursues his prey, and all present cheered her with wonder. She had never danced so elegantly before. Her tender feet felt as if cut with sharp knives, but she cared not for it; a sharper pang had pierced through her heart. She knew this was the last evening she should ever see the prince, for whom she had forsaken her kindred and her home; she had given up her beautiful voice, and suffered unheard-of pain daily for him, while he knew nothing of it. This was the last evening that she would breathe the same air with him, or gaze on the starry sky and the deep sea; an eternal night, without a thought or a dream, awaited her: she had no soul and now she could never win one.

All was joy and gaiety on board the ship till long after midnight; she laughed and danced with the rest, while the thoughts of death were in her heart. The prince kissed his beautiful bride, while she played with his raven hair, till they went arm-in-arm to rest in the splendid tent. Then all became still on board the ship; the helmsman, alone awake, stood at the helm. The little mermaid leaned her white arms on the edge of the vessel, and looked towards the east for the first blush of morning, for that first ray of dawn that would bring her death. She saw her sisters rising out of the flood: they were as pale as herself; but their long beautiful hair waved no more in the wind, and had been cut off.

"We have given our hair to the witch," said they, "to obtain help for you, that you may not die tonight. She has given us a knife: here it is, see it is very sharp. Before the sun rises you must plunge it into the heart of the prince; when the warm blood falls upon your feet they will grow together again, and form into a fish's tail, and you will be once more a mermaid, and return to us to live out your three hundred years before you die and change into the salt sea foam. Haste, then; he or you must die before sunrise. Our old grandmother moans so for you, that her white hair is falling off from sorrow, as ours fell under the witch's scissors. Kill the prince and come back; hasten: do you not see the first red streaks in the sky? In a few minutes the sun will rise, and you must die." And then they sighed deeply and mournfully, and sank down beneath the waves.

The little mermaid drew back the crimson curtain of the tent, and beheld the fair bride with her head resting on the prince's breast. She bent down and kissed his fair brow, then looked at the sky on which the rosy dawn grew brighter and brighter; then she glanced at the sharp knife, and again fixed her eyes on the prince, who whispered the name of his bride in his dreams. She was in his thoughts, and the knife trembled in the hand of the little mermaid: then she flung it far away from her into the waves; the water turned red where it fell, and the drops that spurted up looked like blood. She cast one more lingering, half-fainting glance at the prince, and then threw herself from the ship into the sea, and thought her body was dissolving into foam.

The sun rose above the waves, and his warm rays fell on the cold foam of the little mermaid, who did not feel as if she were dying. She saw the bright sun, and all around her floated hundreds of transparent beautiful beings; she could see through them the white sails of the ship, and the red clouds in the sky; their speech was melodious, but too ethereal to be heard by mortal ears, as they were also unseen by mortal eyes. The little mermaid perceived that she had a body like theirs, and that she continued to rise higher and higher out of the foam. "Where am I?" asked she, and her voice sounded ethereal, as the voice of those who were with her; no earthly music could imitate it.

"Among the daughters of the air," answered one of them. "A mermaid has not an immortal soul, nor can she obtain one unless she wins the love of a human being. On the power of another hangs her eternal destiny. But the daughters of the air, although they do not possess an immortal soul, can, by their good deeds, procure one for themselves. We fly to warm countries, and cool the sultry air that destroys mankind with pestilence. We carry the perfume of the flowers to spread health and restoration. After we have striven for three hundred years to all the good in our power, we receive an immortal soul and take part in the

*She mounted with the other children of the air to a rosy cloud.*

happiness of mankind. You, poor little mermaid, have tried with your whole heart to do as we are doing; you have suffered and endured and raised yourself to the spirit world by your good deeds; and now, by striving for three hundred years in the same way, you may obtain an immortal soul."

The little mermaid lifted her glorified eyes towards the sun, and felt them, for the first time, filling with tears. On the ship, in which she had left the prince, there were life and noise; she saw him and his beautiful bride searching for her; sorrowfully they gazed at the pearly foam, as if they knew she had thrown herself into the waves. Unseen she kissed the forehead of the bride, and fanned the prince, and then mounted with the other children of the air to a rosy cloud that floated through the aether.

"After three hundred years, thus shall we float into the kingdom of heaven," said she. "And we may even get there sooner," whispered one of her companions. "Unseen we can enter the houses of men, where there are children, and for every day on which we find a good child, who is the joy of his parents and deserves their love, our time of probation is shortened. The child does not know, when we fly through the room, that we smile with joy at his good conduct, for we can count one year less of our three hundred years. But when we see a naughty or a wicked child, we shed tears of sorrow, and for every tear a day is added to our time of trial!"

# THE TINDERBOX

A soldier came marching along the high road: "Left, right—left, right." He had his knapsack on his back, and a sword at his side; he had been to the wars, and was now returning home.

As he walked on, he met a very frightful-looking old witch in the road. Her underlip hung quite down on her breast, and she stopped and said, "Good evening, soldier; you have a very fine sword, and a large knapsack, and you are a real soldier; so you shall have as much money as ever you like."

"Thank you, old witch," said the soldier.

"Do you see that large tree?" said the witch, pointing to a tree which stood beside them. "Well, it is quite hollow inside, and you must climb to the top, where you will see a hole, through which you can let yourself down into the tree to a great depth. I will tie a rope around your body, so that I can pull you up again when you call out to me."

"But what am I to do, down there in the tree?" asked the soldier.

"Get money," she replied; "for you must know that when you reach the ground under the tree, you will find yourself in a large hall, lighted up by three hundred lamps; you will then see three doors, which can be easily opened, for the keys are in all the locks. On entering the first of the chambers, to which these doors lead, you will see a large chest, standing in the middle of the floor, and upon it a dog seated, with a pair of eyes as large as teacups. But you need not be at all afraid of him; I will give you my blue checked apron, which you must spread upon the floor, and then boldly seize hold of the dog, and place him upon it. You can then open the chest, and take from it as many pence as you please. They are only copper pence; but if you would rather have silver money, you must go into the second chamber. Here you will find another dog, with eyes as big as mill wheels; but do not let that trouble you. Place him upon my apron, and then take what money you please. If, however, you like gold best, enter the third chamber, where there is another chest full of it. The dog who sits on this chest is very dreadful; his eyes are as big as a tower, but do not mind him. If he also is placed upon my apron, he cannot hurt you, and you may take from the chest what gold you will."

"This is not a bad story," said the soldier; "but what am I to give you, you old witch? For, of course, you do not mean to tell me all this for nothing."

"No," said the witch; "but I do not ask for a single penny. Only promise to bring me an old tinderbox, which my grandmother left behind the last time she went down there."

"Very well; I promise. Now tie the rope around my body."

"Here it is," replied the witch; "and here is my blue checked apron."

As soon as the rope was tied, the soldier climbed up the tree, and let himself down through the hollow to the ground beneath; and here he found, as the witch had told him, a large hall, in which many hundred lamps were all burning. Then he opened the first door. "Ah!" There sat the dog, with the eyes as large as teacups, staring at him.

"You're a pretty fellow," said the soldier, seizing him, and placing him on the witch's apron, while he filled his pockets from the chest with as many pieces as they would hold.

Then he closed the lid, seated the dog upon it again, and walked into another chamber. And, sure enough, there sat the dog with eyes as big as mill wheels.

"You had better not look at me in that way," said the soldier; "you will make your eyes water"; and then he seated him also upon the apron, and opened the chest. But when he saw what a quantity of silver

*There sat the dog, with the eyes as large as teacups, staring at him.*

money it contained, he very quickly threw away all the coppers he had taken, and filled his pockets and his knapsack with nothing but silver.

Then he went into the third room, and there the dog was really hideous; his eyes were truly as big as towers, and they turned around and around in his head like wheels.

"Good morning," said the soldier, touching his cap, for he had never seen such a dog in his life. But after looking at him more closely, he thought he had been civil enough, so he placed him on the floor, and opened the chest. Good gracious, what a quantity of gold there was! Enough to buy all the sugar sticks of the sweet-stuff women; all the tin soldiers, whips, and rocking horses in the world, or even the whole town itself. There was, indeed, an immense quantity. So the soldier now threw away all the silver money he had taken, and filled his pockets and his knapsack with gold instead; and not only his pockets and his knapsack, but even his cap and boots, so that he could scarcely walk.

He was really rich now; so he replaced the dog on the chest, closed the door, and called up through the tree, "Now pull me out, you old witch."

"Have you got the tinderbox?" asked the witch.

"No; I declare I quite forgot it." So he went back and fetched the tinderbox, and then the witch drew him up out of the tree, and he stood again in the high road, with his pockets, his knapsack, his cap, and his boots full of gold.

"What are you going to do with the tinderbox?" asked the soldier.

"That is nothing to you," replied the witch; "you have the money, now give me the tinderbox."

"I tell you what," said the soldier, "if you don't tell me what you are going to do with it, I will draw my sword and cut off your head."

"No," said the witch.

The soldier immediately cut off her head, and there she lay on the ground. Then he tied up all his money in her apron and slung it on his back like a bundle, put the tinderbox in his pocket, and walked off to the nearest town. It was a very nice town, and he put up at the best inn, and ordered a dinner of all his favorite dishes, for now he was rich and had plenty of money.

The servant, who cleaned his boots, thought they certainly were a shabby pair to be worn by such a rich gentleman, for he had not yet bought any new ones. The next day, however, he procured some good clothes and proper boots, so that our soldier soon became known as a fine gentleman, and the people visited him and told him all the wonders that were to be seen in the town, and of the king's beautiful daughter, the princess.

"Where can I see her?" asked the soldier.

"She is not to be seen at all," they said; "she lives in a large copper castle, surrounded by walls and towers. No one but the king himself can pass in or out, for there has been a prophecy that she will marry a common soldier, and the king cannot bear to think of such a marriage."

"I should like very much to see her," thought the soldier; but he could not obtain permission to do so. However, he passed a very pleasant time; went to the theater, drove in the king's garden, and gave a great deal of money to the poor, which was very good of him; he remembered what it had been in olden times to be without a shilling. Now he was rich, had fine clothes, and many friends, who all declared he was a fine fellow and a real gentleman, and all this gratified him exceedingly. But his money would not last forever; and as he spent and gave away a great deal daily, and received none, he found himself at last with only two shillings left. So he was obliged to leave his elegant rooms, and live in a little garret under the roof, where he had to clean his own boots, and even mend them with a large needle. None of his friends came to see him, for there were too many stairs to mount up. One dark evening, he had not even a penny to buy a candle; then all at once he remembered that there was a piece of candle stuck in the tinderbox, which he had brought from the old tree into which the witch had helped him.

He found the tinderbox, but no sooner had he struck a few sparks from the flint and steel than the door flew open and the dog with eyes as big as teacups, whom he had seen while down in the tree, stood before him and said, "What orders, master?"

"Hallo," said the soldier; "well, this is a pleasant tinderbox, if it brings me all I wish for."

"Bring me some money," said he to the dog.

He was gone in a moment, and presently returned, carrying a large bag of coppers in his mouth. The soldier very soon discovered after this the value of the tinderbox. If he struck the flint once, the dog who sat on the chest of copper money made his appearance; if twice, the dog came from the chest of silver; and if three times, the dog with eyes like towers, who watched over the gold. The soldier had now plenty of money; he returned to his elegant rooms, and reappeared in his fine clothes, so that his friends knew him again directly, and made as much of him as before.

After a while he began to think it was very strange that no one could get a look at the princess. "Everyone says she is very beautiful," thought he to himself; "but what is the use of that if she is to be shut up in a copper castle surrounded by so many towers. Can I by any means get to see her? Stop! Where is my tinderbox?"

Then he struck a light, and in a moment the dog, with eyes as big as teacups, stood before him.

"It is midnight," said the soldier, "yet I should very much like to see the princess, if only for a moment."

The dog disappeared instantly, and before the soldier could even look around, he returned with the princess. She was lying on the dog's back asleep, and looked so lovely that everyone who saw her would know she was a real princess. The soldier could not help kissing her, true soldier as he was. Then the dog ran back with the princess; but in the morning, while at breakfast with the king and queen, she told them what a singular dream she had had during the night, of a dog and a soldier, that she had ridden on the dog's back, and been kissed by the soldier.

"That is a very pretty story, indeed," said the queen. So the next night one of the old ladies of the court was set to watch by the princess's bed, to discover whether it really was a dream, or what else it might be.

The soldier longed very much to see the princess once more, so he sent for the dog again in the night to fetch her, and to run with her as fast as ever he could. But the old lady put on galoshes, and ran after him as quickly as he did, and found that he carried the princess into a large house. She thought it would help her to remember the place if she made a large cross on the door with a piece of chalk. Then she went home to bed, and the dog presently returned with the princess. But when he saw that a cross had been made on the door of the house where the soldier lived, he took another piece of chalk and made crosses on all the doors in the town, so that the lady-in-waiting might not be able to find out the right door.

Early the next morning the king and queen accompanied the lady and all the officers of the household to see where the princess had been.

"Here it is," said the king when they came to the first door with a cross on it.

"No, my dear husband, it must be that one," said the queen, pointing to a second door having a cross also.

"And here is one, and there is another!" they all exclaimed; for there were crosses on all the doors in every direction.

So they felt it would be useless to search any farther. But the queen was a very clever woman; she could do a great deal more than merely ride in a carriage. She took her large gold scissors, cut a piece of silk into squares, and made a neat little bag. This bag she filled with buckwheat flour, and tied it around the princess's neck; and then she cut a small hole in the bag, so that the flour might be scattered on the ground as the princess went along. During the night, the dog came again and carried the princess on his back, and ran with her to the soldier, who loved her very much, and wished that he had been a prince, so that he might have her for a wife. The dog did not observe how the flour ran out of the bag all the way from the castle wall to the soldier's house, and even up to the window where he had climbed with the princess. Therefore in the morning the king and queen found out where their daughter had been, and the soldier was taken up and put in prison.

Oh, how dark and disagreeable it was as he sat there, and the people said to him, "Tomorrow you will be hanged." It was not very pleasant news, and besides, he had left the tinderbox at the inn. In the morning he could see through the iron grating of the little window how the people were hastening out of the town to see him hanged; he heard the drums beating, and saw the soldiers marching. Everyone ran out to look at them, and a shoemaker's boy, with a leather apron and slippers on, galloped by so fast that one of his slippers flew off and struck against the wall where the soldier sat looking through the iron grating. "Hallo, you shoemaker's boy, you need not be in such a hurry," cried the soldier to him. "There will be nothing to see till I come; but if you will run to the house where I have been living, and bring me my tinderbox, you shall have four shillings, but you must put your best foot foremost."

The shoemaker's boy liked the idea of getting the four shillings, so he ran very fast and fetched the tinderbox, and gave it to the soldier. And now we shall see what happened. Outside the town a large gibbet had been erected, around which stood the soldiers and several thousands of people. The king and the queen sat on splendid thrones opposite to the judges and the whole council. The soldier already stood on the ladder; but as they were about to place the rope around his neck, he said that an innocent request was often granted to a poor criminal before he suffered death. He wished very much to smoke a pipe, as it would be the last pipe he should ever smoke in the world. The king could not refuse this request, so the soldier took his tinderbox and struck fire once, twice, thrice—and there in a moment stood all the dogs—the one with eyes as big as teacups, the one with eyes as large as mill-wheels, and the third, whose eyes were like towers. "Help me now, that I may not be hanged," cried the soldier.

And the dogs fell upon the judges and all the councillors seized one by the legs and another by the nose, and tossed them many feet high in the air, so that they fell down and were dashed to pieces.

"I will not be touched," said the king. But the largest dog seized him, as well as the queen, and threw them after the others. Then the soldiers and all the people were afraid, and cried, "Good soldier, you shall be our king, and you shall marry the beautiful princess."

So they placed the soldier in the king's carriage, and the three dogs ran on in front and cried "Hurrah!" and the little boys whistled through their fingers, and the soldiers presented arms. The princess came out of the copper castle, and became queen, which was very pleasing to her. The wedding festivities lasted a whole week, and the dogs sat at the table, and stared with all their eyes.

# WHAT THE OLD MAN DOES
# IS ALWAYS RIGHT

I will tell you a story that was told me when I was a little boy. Every time I thought of this story, it seemed to me more and more charming; for it is with stories as it is with many people—they become better as they grow older.

I have no doubt that you have been in the country, and seen a very old farmhouse, with a thatched roof, and mosses and small plants growing wild upon it. There is a stork's nest on the ridge of the gable, for we cannot do without the stork. The walls of the house are sloping, and the windows are low, and only one of the latter is made to open. The baking oven sticks out of the wall like a great knob. An elder tree hangs over the palings, and beneath its branches, at the foot of the paling, is a pool of water, in which a few ducks are amusing themselves. There is a yard dog too, who barks at all corners.

Just such a farmhouse as this stood in a country lane; and in it dwelt an old couple, a peasant and his wife. Small as their possessions were, they had one article they could not do without, and that was a horse, which contrived to live upon the grass which it found by the side of the high road. The old peasant rode into the town upon this horse, and his neighbors often borrowed it of him, and paid for the loan of it by rendering some service to the old couple. After a time they thought it would be as well to sell the horse, or exchange it for something which might be more useful to them. But what might this something be?

"You'll know best, old man," said the wife. "It is fair day today; so ride into town, and get rid of the horse for money, or make a good exchange; whichever you do will be right to me, so ride to the fair."

And she fastened his neckerchief for him; for she could do that better than he could, and she could also tie it very prettily in a double bow. She also smoothed his hat around and around with the palm of her hand, and gave him a kiss. Then he rode away upon the horse that was to be sold or bartered for something else. Yes, the old man knew what he was about. The sun shone with great heat, and not a cloud was to be seen in the sky. The road was very dusty; for a number of people, all going to the fair, were driving, riding, or walking upon it. There was no shelter anywhere from the hot sunshine. Among the rest a man came trudging along, and driving a cow to the fair. The cow was as beautiful a creature as any cow could be.

"She gives good milk, I am certain," said the peasant to himself. "That would be a very good exchange: the cow for the horse. Hallo there! You with the cow," he said. "I tell you what; I dare say a horse is of more value than a cow; but I don't care about that—a cow will be more useful to me; so, if you like, we'll exchange."

"To be sure I will," said the man.

Accordingly the exchange was made; and as the matter was settled, the peasant might have turned back; for he had done the business he came to do. But, having made up his mind to go to the fair, he determined to do so, if only to have a look at it; so on he went to the town with his cow. Leading the animal, he strode on sturdily, and, after a short time, overtook a man who was driving a sheep. It was a good fat sheep, with a fine fleece on its back.

"I should like to have that fellow," said the peasant to himself. "There is plenty of grass for him by our palings, and in the winter we could keep him in the room with us. Perhaps it would be more profitable to have a sheep than a cow. Shall I exchange?"

The man with the sheep was quite ready, and the bargain was quickly made. And then our peasant continued his way on the high road with his sheep. Soon after this, he overtook another man, who had come into the road from a field, and was carrying a large goose under his arm.

"What a heavy creature you have there!" said the peasant. "It has plenty of feathers and plenty of fat, and would look well tied to a string, or paddling in the water at our place. That would be very useful to my old woman; she could make all sorts of profits out of it. How often she has said, 'If we only had a goose!' Now here is an opportunity, and, if possible, I will get it for her. Shall we exchange? I will give you my sheep for your goose, and my thanks into the bargain."

The other had not the least objection, and accordingly the exchange was made, and our peasant became possessor of the goose. By this time he had arrived very near the town. The crowd on the high road had been gradually increasing, and there was quite a rush of men and cattle. The cattle walked on the path and by the palings, and at the turnpike gate they even walked into the tollkeeper's potato field, where one fowl was strutting about with a string tied to its leg, for fear it should take fright at the crowd, and run away and get lost. The tail feathers of the fowl were very short, and it winked with both its eyes, and looked very cunning as it said "Cluck, cluck."

What were the thoughts of the fowl as it said this I cannot tell you; but directly our good man saw it, he thought, "Why, that's the finest fowl I ever saw in my life; it's finer than our parson's brood hen, upon my word. I should like to have that fowl. Fowls can always pick up a few grains that lie about, and almost keep themselves. I think it would be a good exchange if I could get it for my goose. Shall we exchange?" he asked the tollkeeper.

"Exchange," repeated the man; "well, it would not be a bad thing."

And so they made an exchange—the tollkeeper at the turnpike gate kept the goose, and the peasant carried off the fowl. Now he had really done a great deal of business on his way to the fair, and he was hot and tired. He wanted something to eat, and a glass of ale to refresh himself;

so he turned his steps to an inn. He was just about to enter when the ostler came out, and they met at the door. The ostler was carrying a sack. "What have you in that sack?" asked the peasant.

"Rotten apples," answered the ostler; "a whole sackful of them. They will do to feed the pigs with."

"Why, that will be terrible waste," he replied; "I should like to take them home to my old woman. Last year the old apple tree by the grass plot only bore one apple, and we kept it in the cupboard till it was quite withered and rotten. It was always property, my old woman said; and here she would see a great deal of property—a whole sackful; I should like to show them to her."

"What will you give me for the sackful?" asked the ostler.

"What will I give? Well, I will give you my fowl in exchange."

So he gave up the fowl, and received the apples, which he carried into the inn parlor. He leaned the sack carefully against the stove, and then went to the table. But the stove was hot, and he had not thought of that. Many guests were present—horse dealers, cattle drovers, and two Englishmen. The Englishmen were so rich that their pockets quite bulged out and seemed ready to burst; and they could bet too, as you shall hear.

"Hiss-s-s, hiss-s-s." What could that be by the stove? The apples were beginning to roast.

"What is that?" asked one.

"Why, do you know—" said our peasant, and then he told them the whole story of the horse, which he had exchanged for a cow, and all the rest of it, down to the apples.

"Well, your old woman will give it you well when you get home," said one of the Englishmen. "Won't there be a noise?"

"What! Give me what?" said the peasant. "Why, she will kiss me, and say, 'What the old man does is always right.'"

"Let us lay a wager on it," said the Englishmen. "We'll wager you a ton of coined gold, a hundred pounds to the hundredweight."

"No; a bushel will be enough," replied the peasant. "I can only set a bushel of apples against it, and I'll throw myself and my old woman into the bargain; that will pile up the measure, I fancy."

"Done! Taken!" And so the bet was made.

Then the landlord's coach came to the door, and the two Englishmen and the peasant got in, and away they drove, and soon arrived and stopped at the peasant's hut. "Good evening, old woman." "Good evening, old man." "I've made the exchange."

"Ah, well, you understand what you're about," said the woman. Then she embraced him, and paid no attention to the strangers, nor did she notice the sack.

"I got a cow in exchange for the horse."

"Thank heaven," said she. "Now we shall have plenty of milk, and butter, and cheese on the table. That was a capital exchange."

"Yes, but I changed the cow for a sheep."

"Ah, better still!" cried the wife. "You always think of everything; we have just enough pasture for a sheep. Ewe's milk and cheese, woollen jackets and stockings! The cow could not give all these, and her hair only falls off. How you think of everything!"

"But I changed away the sheep for a goose."

"Then we shall have roast goose to eat this year. You dear old man, you are always thinking of something to please me. This is delightful. We can let the goose walk about with a string tied to her leg, so she will be fatter still before we roast her."

"But I gave away the goose for a fowl."

"A fowl! Well, that was a good exchange," replied the woman. "The fowl will lay eggs and hatch them, and we shall have chickens; we shall soon have a poultry yard. Oh, this is just what I was wishing for."

"Yes, but I exchanged the fowl for a sack of shriveled apples."

"What! I really must give you a kiss for that!" exclaimed the wife. "My dear, good husband, now I'll tell you something. Do you know, almost as soon as you left me this morning, I began to think of what I could give you nice for supper this evening, and then I thought of fried eggs and bacon, with sweet herbs; I had eggs and bacon, but I wanted the herbs; so I went over to the schoolmaster's: I knew they had plenty of herbs, but the schoolmistress is very mean, although she can smile so sweetly. I begged her to lend me a handful of herbs. 'Lend!' she exclaimed, 'I have nothing to lend; nothing at all grows in our garden, not even a shriveled apple; I could not even lend you a shriveled apple, my dear woman.' But now I can lend her ten, or a whole sackful, which I'm very glad of; it makes me laugh to think about it"; and then she gave him a hearty kiss.

"Well, I like all this," said both the Englishmen; "always going down the hill, and yet always merry; it's worth the money to see it." So they paid a hundredweight of gold to the peasant, who, whatever he did, was not scolded but kissed.

Yes, it always pays best when the wife sees and maintains that her husband knows best, and whatever he does is right.

That is a story which I heard when I was a child; and now you have heard it too, and know that "What the old man does is always right."

# THE LITTLE MATCH GIRL

It was terribly cold and nearly dark on the last evening of the old year, and the snow was falling fast. In the cold and the darkness, a poor little girl, with bare head and naked feet, roamed through the streets. It is true she had on a pair of slippers when she left home, but they were not of much use. They were very large—so large, indeed, that they had belonged to her mother, and the poor little creature had lost them in running across the street to avoid two carriages that were rolling along at a terrible rate. One of the slippers she could not find, and a boy seized upon the other and ran away with it, saying that he could use it as a cradle, when he had children of his own. So the little girl went on with her little naked feet, which were quite red and blue with the cold. In an old apron she carried a number of matches, and had a bundle of them in her hands. No one had bought anything of her the whole day, nor had anyone given her even a penny. Shivering with cold and hunger, she crept along; poor little child, she looked the picture of misery. The snowflakes fell on her long, fair hair, which hung in curls on her shoulders, but she regarded them not.

Lights were shining from every window, and there was a savory smell of roast goose, for it was New Year's Eve—yes, she remembered that. In a corner, between two houses, one of which projected beyond the other, she sank down and huddled herself together. She had drawn her little feet under her, but she could not keep off the cold; and she dared not go home, for she had sold no matches, and could not take home even a penny of money. Her father would certainly beat her;

besides, it was almost as cold at home as here, for they had only the roof to cover them, through which the wind howled, although the largest holes had been stopped up with straw and rags. Her little hands were almost frozen with the cold. Ah! Perhaps a burning match might be some good, if she could draw it from the bundle and strike it against the wall, just to warm her fingers. She drew one out—"scratch!"—how it sputtered as it burned! It gave a warm, bright light, like a little candle, as she held her hand over it. It was really a wonderful light. It seemed to the little girl that she was sitting by a large iron stove with polished brass feet and a brass ornament. How the fire burned, and seemed so beautifully warm that the child stretched out her feet as if to warm them when—lo!—the flame of the match went out, the stove vanished, and she had only the remains of the half-burned match in her hand.

She rubbed another match on the wall. It burst into a flame, and where its light fell upon the wall it became as transparent as a veil, and she could see into the room. The table was covered with a snowy white tablecloth, on which stood a splendid dinner service, and a steaming roast goose, stuffed with apples and dried plums. And what was still more wonderful, the goose jumped down from the dish and waddled across the floor, with a knife and fork in its breast, to the little girl. Then the match went out, and there remained nothing but the thick, damp, cold wall before her.

She lighted another match, and then she found herself sitting under a beautiful Christmas tree. It was larger and more beautifully decorated than the one which she had seen through the glass door at the rich merchant's. Thousands of tapers were burning upon the green branches, and colored pictures, like those she had seen in the show windows, looked down upon it all. The little one stretched out her hand towards them, and the match went out.

The Christmas lights rose higher and higher, till they looked to her like the stars in the sky. Then she saw a star fall, leaving behind it

*She found herself sitting under a beautiful Christmas tree.*

a bright streak of fire. "Someone is dying," thought the little girl, for her old grandmother, the only one who had ever loved her, and who was now dead, had told her that when a star falls, a soul was going up to God.

She again rubbed a match on the wall, and the light shone around her; in the brightness stood her old grandmother, clear and shining, yet mild and loving in her appearance.

"Grandmother," cried the little one, "O take me with you; I know you will go away when the match burns out; you will vanish like the warm stove, the roast goose, and the large, glorious Christmas tree." And she made haste to light the whole bundle of matches, for she wished to keep her grandmother there. And the matches glowed with a light that was brighter than the noonday, and her grandmother had never appeared so large or so beautiful. She took the little girl in her arms, and they both flew upwards in brightness and joy far above the earth, where there was neither cold nor hunger nor pain, for they were with God.

In the dawn of morning there lay the poor little one, with pale cheeks and smiling mouth, leaning against the wall; she had been frozen to death on the last evening of the year, and the New Year's sun rose and shone upon a little corpse! The child still sat, in the stiffness of death, holding the matches in her hand, one bundle of which was burned. "She tried to warm herself," said some. No one imagined what beautiful things she had seen, nor into what glory she had entered with her grandmother, on New Year's Day.

# LITTLE CLAUS AND BIG CLAUS

In a village there once lived two men who had the same name. They were both called Claus. One of them had four horses, but the other had only one; so to distinguish them, people called the owner of the four horses "Great Claus," and he who had only one "Little Claus." Now we shall hear what happened to them, for this is a true story.

Through the whole week, Little Claus was obliged to plow for Great Claus, and lend him his one horse; and once a week, on a Sunday, Great Claus lent him all his four horses. Then how Little Claus would smack his whip over all five horses—they were as good as his own on that one day. The sun shone brightly, and the church bells were ringing merrily as the people passed by, dressed in their best clothes, with their prayer books under their arms. They were going to hear the clergyman preach. They looked at Little Claus plowing with his five horses, and he was so proud that he smacked his whip and said, "Gee-up, my five horses."

"You must not say that," said Big Claus; "for only one of them belongs to you."

But Little Claus soon forgot what he ought to say, and when anyone passed he would call out, "Gee-up, my five horses!"

"Now I must beg you not to say that again," said Big Claus; "for if you do, I shall hit your horse on the head, so that he will drop dead on the spot, and there will be an end to him."

"I promise you I will not say it anymore," said the other; but as soon as people came by, nodding to him, and wishing him "Good day," he became so pleased, and thought how grand it looked to have five horses plowing in his field, that he cried out again, "Gee-up, all my horses!"

"I'll gee-up your horses for you," said Big Claus; and seizing a hammer, he struck the one horse of Little Claus on the head, and he fell dead instantly.

"Oh, now I have no horse at all," said Little Claus, weeping. But after a while he took off the dead horse's skin, and hung the hide to dry in the wind. Then he put the dry skin into a bag, and, placing it over his shoulder, went out into the next town to sell the horse's skin. He had a very long way to go, and had to pass through a dark, gloomy forest. Presently a storm arose, and he lost his way, and before he discovered the right path, evening came on, and it was still a long way to the town, and too far to return home before night. Near the road stood a large farmhouse. The shutters outside the windows were closed, but lights shone through the crevices at the top.

"I might get permission to stay here for the night," thought Little Claus; so he went up to the door and knocked. The farmer's wife opened the door; but when she heard what he wanted, she told him to go away, as her husband would not allow her to admit strangers. "Then I shall be obliged to lie out here," said Little Claus to himself, as the farmer's wife shut the door in his face. Near to the farmhouse stood a large haystack, and between it and the house was a small shed, with a thatched roof. "I can lie up there," said Little Claus, as he saw the roof; "it will make a famous bed, but I hope the stork will not fly down and bite my legs"; for on it stood a living stork, whose nest was in the roof.

So Little Claus climbed to the roof of the shed, and while he turned himself to get comfortable, he discovered that the wooden shutters, which were closed, did not reach to the tops of the windows of the farmhouse, so that he could see into a room, in which a large table was laid out with wine, roast meat, and a splendid fish. The farmer's wife and the sexton were sitting at the table together; and she filled his glass, and helped him plenteously to fish, which appeared to be his favorite dish. "If I could only get some, too," thought Little Claus; and then, as he stretched his neck towards the window he spied a large, beautiful pie—indeed they had a glorious feast before them.

At this moment he heard someone riding down the road towards the farmhouse. It was the farmer returning home. He was a good man, but still he had a very strange prejudice—he could not bear the sight of a sexton. If one appeared before him, he would put himself in a terrible rage. In consequence of this dislike, the sexton had gone to visit the farmer's wife during her husband's absence from home, and the good woman had placed before him the best she had in the house to eat. When she heard the farmer coming she was frightened, and begged the sexton to hide himself in a large empty chest that stood in the room. He did so, for he knew her husband could not endure the sight of a sexton. The woman then quickly put away the wine, and hid all the rest of the nice things in the oven; for if her husband had seen them he would have asked what they were brought out for.

"Oh, dear," sighed Little Claus from the top of the shed, as he saw all the good things disappear.

"Is anyone up there?" asked the farmer, looking up and discovering Little Claus. "Why are you lying up there? Come down, and come into the house with me." So Little Claus came down and told the farmer how he had lost his way and begged for a night's lodging.

"All right," said the farmer; "but we must have something to eat first."

The woman received them both very kindly, laid the cloth on a large table, and placed before them a dish of porridge. The farmer was very hungry, and ate his porridge with a good appetite, but Little Claus could not help thinking of the nice roast meat, fish, and pies, which he knew were in the oven. Under the table, at his feet, lay the sack containing the horse's skin, which he intended to sell at the next town. Now Little Claus did not relish the porridge at all, so he trod with his foot on the sack under the table, and the dry skin squeaked quite loud. "Hush!" said Little Claus to his sack, at the same time treading upon it again, till it squeaked louder than before.

"Hallo! What have you got in your sack?" asked the farmer.

"Oh, it is a conjuror," said Little Claus; "and he says we need not eat porridge, for he has conjured the oven full of roast meat, fish, and pie."

"Wonderful!" cried the farmer, starting up and opening the oven door; and there lay all the nice things hidden by the farmer's wife, but which he supposed had been conjured there by the wizard under the table. The woman dared not say anything; so she placed the things before them, and they both ate of the fish, the meat, and the pastry.

Then Little Claus trod again upon his sack, and it squeaked as before. "What does he say now?" asked the farmer.

"He says," replied Little Claus, "that there are three bottles of wine for us, standing in the corner, by the oven."

So the woman was obliged to bring out the wine also, which she had hidden, and the farmer drank it till he became quite merry. He would have liked such a conjuror as Little Claus carried in his sack. "Could he conjure up the evil one?" asked the farmer. "I should like to see him now, while I am so merry."

"Oh, yes!" replied Little Claus. "My conjuror can do anything I ask him—can you not?" he asked, treading at the same time on the sack till it squeaked. "Do you hear? He answers 'Yes,' but he fears that we shall not like to look at him."

"Oh, I am not afraid. What will he be like?"

"Well, he is very much like a sexton."

"Ha!" said the farmer. "Then he must be ugly. Do you know I cannot endure the sight of a sexton? However, that doesn't matter, I shall know who it is; so I shall not mind. Now then, I have got up my courage, but don't let him come too near me."

"Stop, I must ask the conjuror," said Little Claus; so he trod on the bag, and stooped his ear down to listen.

*"Hallo! What have you got in your sack?" asked the farmer.*

"What does he say?"

"He says that you must go and open that large chest which stands in the corner, and you will see the evil one crouching down inside; but you must hold the lid firmly, that he may not slip out."

"Will you come and help me hold it?" said the farmer, going towards the chest in which his wife had hidden the sexton, who now lay inside, very much frightened. The farmer opened the lid a very little way, and peeped in.

"Oh," cried he, springing backwards, "I saw him, and he is exactly like our sexton. How dreadful it is!" So after that he was obliged to drink again, and they sat and drank till far into the night.

"You must sell your conjuror to me," said the farmer; "ask as much as you like, I will pay it; indeed I would give you directly a whole bushel of gold."

"No, indeed, I cannot," said Little Claus; "only think how much profit I could make out of this conjuror."

"But I should like to have him," said the fanner, still continuing his entreaties.

"Well," said Little Claus at length, "you have been so good as to give me a night's lodging, I will not refuse you; you shall have the conjuror for a bushel of money, but I will have quite full measure."

"So you shall," said the farmer; "but you must take away the chest as well. I would not have it in the house another hour; there is no knowing if he may not be still there."

So Little Claus gave the farmer the sack containing the dried horse's skin, and received in exchange a bushel of money—full measure. The farmer also gave him a wheelbarrow on which to carry away the chest and the gold.

"Farewell," said Little Claus, as he went off with his money and the great chest, in which the sexton lay still concealed. On one side of the forest was a broad, deep river. The water flowed so rapidly that very few were able to swim against the stream. A new bridge had lately been built across it, and in the middle of this bridge Little Claus stopped, and said, loud enough to be heard by the sexton, "Now what shall I do with this stupid chest; it is as heavy as if it were full of stones: I shall be tired if I roll it any farther, so I may as well throw it in the river; if it swims after me to my house, well and good, and if not, it will not much matter."

So he seized the chest in his hand and lifted it up a little, as if he were going to throw it into the water.

"No, leave it alone," cried the sexton from within the chest; "let me out first."

"Oh," exclaimed Little Claus, pretending to be frightened, "he is in there still, is he? I must throw him into the river, that he may be drowned."

"Oh, no; oh, no," cried the sexton; "I will give you a whole bushel full of money if you will let me go."

"Why, that is another matter," said Little Claus, opening the chest. The sexton crept out, pushed the empty chest into the water, and went to his house, then he measured out a whole bushel full of gold for Little Claus, who had already received one from the farmer, so that now he had a barrow full.

"I have been well paid for my horse," said he to himself when he reached home, entered his own room, and emptied all his money into a heap on the floor. "How vexed Great Claus will be when he finds out how rich I have become all through my one horse; but I shall not tell him exactly how it all happened." Then he sent a boy to Great Claus to borrow a bushel measure.

"What can he want it for?" thought Great Claus; so he smeared the bottom of the measure with tar, that some of whatever was put into it might stick there and remain. And so it happened; for when the measure returned, three new silver florins were sticking to it.

"What does this mean?" said Great Claus; so he ran off directly to Little Claus, and asked, "Where did you get so much money?"

"Oh, for my horse's skin: I sold it yesterday."

"It was certainly well paid for then," said Great Claus; and he ran home to his house, seized a hatchet, and knocked all his four horses on the head, flayed off their skins, and took them to the town to sell. "Skins, skins, who'll buy skins?" he cried, as he went through the streets. All the shoemakers and tanners came running, and asked how much he wanted for them.

"A bushel of money, for each," replied Great Claus.

"Are you mad?" they all cried; "do you think we have money to spend by the bushel?"

"Skins, skins," he cried again, "who'll buy skins?" But to all who inquired the price, his answer was, "A bushel of money."

"He is making fools of us," said they all; then the shoemakers took their straps, and the tanners their leather aprons, and began to beat Great Claus.

"Skins, skins!" they cried, mocking him. "Yes, we'll mark your skin for you, till it is black and blue."

"Out of the town with him," said they. And Great Claus was obliged to run as fast as he could—he had never before been so thoroughly beaten.

"Ah," said he, as he came to his house; "Little Claus shall pay me for this; I will beat him to death."

Meanwhile, the old grandmother of Little Claus died. She had been cross, unkind, and really spiteful to him; but he was very sorry, and took the dead woman and laid her in his warm bed to see if he could bring her to life again. There he determined that she should lie the whole night, while he seated himself in a chair in a corner of the room as he had often done before.

During the night, as he sat there, the door opened, and in came Great Claus with a hatchet. He knew well where Little Claus's bed stood; so he went right up to it, and struck the old grandmother on the head, thinking it must be Little Claus.

"There," cried he, "now you cannot make a fool of me again"; and then he went home.

"That is a very wicked man," thought Little Claus; "he meant to kill me. It is a good thing for my old grandmother that she was already dead, or he would have taken her life." Then he dressed his old grandmother in her best clothes, borrowed a horse of his neighbor, and harnessed it to a cart. Then he placed the old woman on the back seat, so that she might not fall out as he drove, and rode away through the wood. By sunrise they reached a large inn, where Little Claus stopped and went to get something to eat. The landlord was a rich man, and a good man too; but as passionate as if he had been made of pepper and snuff.

"Good morning," said he to Little Claus; "you are come betimes today."

"Yes," said Little Claus; "I am going to the town with my old grandmother; she is sitting at the back of the wagon, but I cannot bring her into the room. Will you take her a glass of mead? But you must speak very loud, for she cannot hear well."

"Yes, certainly I will," replied the landlord; and, pouring out a glass of mead, he carried it out to the dead grandmother, who sat upright in the cart.

"Here is a glass of mead from your grandson," said the landlord. The dead woman did not answer a word, but sat quite still.

"Do you not hear?" cried the landlord as loud as he could. "Here is a glass of mead from your grandson."

Again and again he bawled it out, but as she did not stir he flew into a passion, and threw the glass of mead in her face; it struck her on the nose, and she fell backwards out of the cart, for she was only seated there, not tied in.

"Hallo!" cried Little Claus, rushing out of the door, and seizing hold of the landlord by the throat. "You have killed my grandmother; see, here is a great hole in her forehead."

"Oh, how unfortunate," said the landlord, wringing his hands. "This all comes of my fiery temper. Dear Little Claus, I will give you a bushel of money; I will bury your grandmother as if she were my own; only keep silent, or else they will cut off my head, and that would be disagreeable."

So it happened that Little Claus received another bushel of money, and the landlord buried his old grandmother as if she had been his own. When Little Claus reached home again, he immediately sent a boy to Great Claus, requesting him to lend him a bushel measure. "How is this?" thought Great Claus. "Did I not kill him? I must go and see for myself." So he went to Little Claus, and took the bushel measure with him. "How did you get all this money?" asked Great Claus, staring with wide-open eyes at his neighbor's treasures.

"You killed my grandmother instead of me," said Little Claus; "so I have sold her for a bushel of money."

"That is a good price at all events," said Great Claus. So he went home, took a hatchet, and killed his old grandmother with one blow. Then he placed her on a cart, and drove into the town to the apothecary, and asked him if he would buy a dead body.

"Whose is it, and where did you get it?" asked the apothecary.

"It is my grandmother," he replied; "I killed her with a blow, that I might get a bushel of money for her."

"Heaven preserve us!" cried the apothecary. "You are out of your mind. Don't say such things, or you will lose your head." And then he talked to him seriously about the wicked deed he had done, and told him that such a wicked man would surely be punished. Great Claus got so frightened that he rushed out of the surgery, jumped into the cart, whipped up his horses, and drove home quickly. The apothecary and all the people thought him mad, and let him drive where he liked.

"You shall pay for this," said Great Claus, as soon as he got into the high road, "that you shall, Little Claus." So as soon as he reached home he took the largest sack he could find and went over to Little Claus.

"You have played me another trick," said he. "First, I killed all my horses, and then my old grandmother, and it is all your fault; but you shall not make a fool of me anymore." So he laid hold of Little Claus around the body, and pushed him into the sack, which he took on his shoulders, saying, "Now I'm going to drown you in the river."

He had a long way to go before he reached the river, and Little Claus was not a very light weight to carry. The road led by the church, and as they passed he could hear the organ playing and the people singing beautifully. Great Claus put down the sack close to the church door, and thought he might as well go in and hear a psalm before he went any farther. Little Claus could not possibly get out of the sack, and all the people were in church; so in he went.

"Oh dear, oh dear," sighed Little Claus in the sack, as he turned and twisted about; but he found he could not loosen the string with which it was tied. Presently an old cattle driver with snowy hair passed by, carrying a large staff in his hand, with which he drove a large herd of cows and oxen before him. They stumbled against the sack in which lay Little Claus, and turned it over. "Oh dear," sighed Little Claus, "I am very young, yet I am soon going to heaven."

"And I, poor fellow," said the cattle driver, "I who am so old already, cannot get there."

"Open the sack," cried Little Claus; "creep into it instead of me, and you will soon be there."

"With all my heart," replied the drover, opening the sack, from which sprung Little Claus as quickly as possible. "Will you take care of my cattle?" said the old man, as he crept into the bag.

"Yes," said Little Claus, and he tied up the sack, and then walked off with all the cows and oxen.

When Great Claus came out of church, he took up the sack and placed it on his shoulders. It appeared to have become lighter, for the old drover was not half so heavy as Little Claus.

"How light he seems now," said he. "Ah, it is because I have been to a church."

So he walked on to the river, which was deep and broad, and threw the sack containing the old drover into the water, believing it to be Little Claus. "There you may lie!" he exclaimed. "You will play me no more tricks now." Then he turned to go home, but when he came to a place where two roads crossed, there was Little Claus driving the cattle. "How is this?" said Great Claus. "Did I not drown you just now?"

"Yes," said Little Claus; "you threw me into the river about half an hour ago."

"But wherever did you get all these fine beasts?" asked Great Claus.

"These beasts are sea cattle," replied Little Claus. "I'll tell you the whole story, and thank you for drowning me; I am above you now, for I am really very rich. I was frightened, to be sure, while I lay tied up in the sack, and the wind whistled in my ears when you threw me into the river from the bridge, and I sank to the bottom immediately; but I did not hurt myself, for I fell upon beautifully soft grass which grows down there; and in a moment, the sack opened, and the sweetest little maiden came towards me. She had snow-white robes, and a wreath of green leaves on her wet hair. She took me by the hand and said, 'So you are come, Little Claus, and here are some cattle for you to begin with. About a mile farther on the road, there is another herd for you.'

"Then I saw that the river formed a great highway for the people who live in the sea. They were walking and driving here and there from the sea to the land at the spot where the river terminates. The bed of the river was covered with the loveliest flowers and sweet fresh grass. The fish swam past me as rapidly as the birds do here in the air. How handsome all the people were, and what fine cattle were grazing on the hills and in the valleys!"

"But why did you come up again," said Great Claus, "if it was all so beautiful down there? I should not have done so!"

"Well," said Little Claus, "it was good policy on my part; you heard me say just now that I was told by the sea maiden to go a mile farther on the road, and I should find a whole herd of cattle. By the road she meant the river, for she could not travel any other way; but I knew the winding of the river, and how it bends, sometimes to the right and sometimes to the left, and it seemed a long way, so I chose a shorter one; and, by coming up to the land, and then driving across the fields back again to the river, I shall save half a mile, and get all my cattle more quickly."

"What a lucky fellow you are!" exclaimed Great Claus. "Do you think I should get any sea cattle if I went down to the bottom of the river?"

"Yes, I think so," said Little Claus; "but I cannot carry you there in a sack, you are too heavy. However if you will go there first, and then creep into a sack, I will throw you in with the greatest pleasure."

"Thank you," said Great Claus; "but remember, if I do not get any sea cattle down there, I shall come up again and give you a good thrashing."

"No, now, don't be too fierce about it!" said Little Claus, as they walked on towards the river. When they approached it, the cattle, who were very thirsty, saw the stream, and ran down to drink.

"See what a hurry they are in," said Little Claus, "they are longing to get down again."

"Come, help me, make haste," said Great Claus; "or you'll get beaten."

So he crept into a large sack, which had been lying across the back of one of the oxen.

"Put in a stone," said Great Claus, "or I may not sink."

"Oh, there's not much fear of that," he replied; still he put a large stone into the bag, and then tied it tightly, and gave it a push.

"Plump!" In went Great Claus, and immediately sank to the bottom of the river.

"I'm afraid he will not find any cattle," said Little Claus, and then he drove his own beasts homewards.

# THE SHEPHERDESS AND THE CHIMNEY SWEEP

Have you ever seen an old wooden cupboard quite black with age, and ornamented with carved foliage and curious figures? Well, just such a cupboard stood in a parlor, and had been left to the family as a legacy by the great-grandmother. It was covered from top to bottom with carved roses and tulips; the most curious scrolls were drawn upon it, and out of them peeped little stags' heads, with antlers. In the middle of the cupboard door was the carved figure of a man most ridiculous to look at. He grinned at you, for no one could call it laughing. He had goat's legs, little horns on his head, and a long beard; the children in the room always called him, "Major-general-field-sergeant-commander Billy-goat's-legs." It was certainly a very difficult name to pronounce, and there are very few who ever receive such a title, but then it seemed wonderful how he came to be carved at all; yet there he was, always looking at the table under the looking-glass, where stood a very pretty little shepherdess made of china. Her shoes were gilt, and her dress had a red rose for an ornament. She wore a hat, and carried a crook, that were both gilded, and looked very bright and pretty.

Close by her side stood a little chimney sweep, as black as coal, and also made of china. He was, however, quite as clean and neat as any other china figure; he only represented a black chimney sweep, and the china workers might just as well have made him a prince, had they felt inclined to do so. He stood holding his ladder quite handily, and his face was as fair and rosy as a girl's—indeed, that was rather a mistake as it should have had some black marks on it.

He and the shepherdess had been placed close together, side by side; and, being so placed, they became engaged to each other, for they were very well suited, being both made of the same sort of china, and being equally fragile. Close to them stood another figure, three times as large as they were, and also made of china. He was an old Chinaman, who could nod his head, and used to pretend that he was the grandfather of the shepherdess, although he could not prove it. He however assumed authority over her, and therefore when "Major-general-field-sergeant-commander Billy-goat's-legs" asked for the little shepherdess to be his wife, he nodded his head to show that he consented.

"You will have a husband," said the old Chinaman to her, "who I really believe is made of mahogany. You will be the wife of Major-general-field-sergeant-commander Billy-goat's-legs. He has the whole cupboard full of silver plate, which he keeps locked up in secret drawers."

"I won't go into the dark cupboard," said the little shepherdess. "I have heard that he has eleven china wives there already."

"Then you shall be the twelfth," said the old Chinaman. "Tonight as soon as you hear a rattling in the old cupboard, you shall be married, as true as I am a Chinaman," and then he nodded his head and fell asleep.

Then the little shepherdess cried, and looked at her sweetheart, the china chimney sweep. "I must entreat you," said she, "to go out with me into the wide world, for we cannot stay here."

"I will do whatever you wish," said the little chimney sweep; "let us go immediately: I think I shall be able to maintain you with my profession."

"If we were but safely down from the table!" said she. "I shall not be happy till we are really out in the world."

Then he comforted her, and showed her how to place her little foot on the carved edge and gilt-leaf ornaments of the table. He brought his little ladder to help her, and so they contrived to reach the floor. But when they looked at the old cupboard, they saw it was all in an uproar. The carved stags pushed out their heads, raised their antlers, and twisted their necks. The major-general sprung up in the air, and cried out to the old Chinaman, "They are running away! They are running away!"

The two were rather frightened at this, so they jumped into the drawer of the window-seat. Here were three or four packs of cards not quite complete, and a doll's theater, which had been built up very neatly. A comedy was being performed in it, and all the queens of diamonds, clubs, hearts, and spades, sat in the first row fanning themselves with tulips, and behind them stood all the knaves, showing that they had heads above and below as playing cards generally have. The play was about two lovers, who were not allowed to marry, and the shepherdess wept because it was so like her own story. "I cannot bear it," said she, "I must get out of the drawer"; but when they reached the floor and cast their eyes on the table, there was the old Chinaman awake and shaking his whole body, till all at once down he came on the floor, "plump." "The old Chinaman is coming," cried the little shepherdess in a fright, and down she fell on one knee.

"I have thought of something," said the chimney sweep; "let us get into the great potpourri jar which stands in the corner; there we can lie on rose leaves and lavender, and throw salt in his eyes if he comes near us."

"No, that will never do," said she, "because I know that the Chinaman and the potpourri jar were lovers once, and there always remains behind a feeling of goodwill between those who have been as intimate as that. No, there is nothing left for us but to go out into the wide world."

"Have you really courage enough to go out into the wide world with me?" said the chimney sweep. "Have you thought how large it is, and that we can never come back here again?"

"Yes, I have," she replied.

When the chimney-sweep saw that she was quite firm, he said, "My way is through the stove and up the chimney. Have you courage to creep with me through the fire box and the iron pipe? When we get to the chimney I shall know how to manage very well. We shall soon climb too high for anyone to reach us, and we shall come through a hole in the top out into the wide world."

So he led her to the door of the stove.

"It looks very dark," said she; still she went in with him through the stove and through the pipe, where it was as dark as pitch.

"Now we are in the chimney," said he; "and look, there is a beautiful star shining above it." It was a real star shining down upon them as if it would show them the way. So they clambered, and crept on, and a frightful steep place it was; but the chimney sweep helped her and supported her, till they got higher and higher. He showed her the best places on which to set her little china feet, so at last they reached the top of the chimney, and sat themselves down, for they were very tired, as may be supposed. The sky, with all its stars, was over their heads, and below were the roofs of the town. They could see for a very long distance out into the wide world, and the poor little shepherdess leaned her head on her chimney sweep's shoulder, and wept till she washed the gilt off her sash; the world was so different to what she expected.

"This is too much," she said; "I cannot bear it, the world is too large. Oh, I wish I were safe back on the table again, under the looking-glass; I shall never be happy till I am safe back again. Now I have followed you out into the wide world, you will take me back, if you love me."

Then the chimney sweep tried to reason with her, and spoke of the old Chinaman, and of Major-general-field-sergeant-commander Billy-goat's-legs; but she sobbed so bitterly, and kissed her little chimney sweep till he was obliged to do all she asked, foolish as it was. And so, with a great deal of trouble, they climbed down the chimney, and then crept through the pipe and stove, which were certainly not very pleasant places. Then they stood in the dark firebox and listened behind the door to hear what was going on in the room. As it was all quiet, they peeped out. Alas! There lay the old Chinaman on the floor; he had fallen down from the table as he attempted to run after them, and was broken into three pieces; his back had separated entirely, and his head had rolled into a corner of the room. The major-general stood in his old place, and appeared lost in thought.

"This is terrible," said the little shepherdess. "My poor old grandfather is broken to pieces, and it is our fault. I shall never live after this," and she wrung her little hands.

"He can be riveted," said the chimney sweep; "he can be riveted. Do not be so hasty. If they cement his back, and put a good rivet in it, he will be as good as new, and be able to say as many disagreeable things to us as ever."

"Do you think so?" said she; and then they climbed up to the table, and stood in their old places.

"As we have done no good," said the chimney sweep, "we might as well have remained here, instead of taking so much trouble."

"I wish grandfather was riveted," said the shepherdess. "Will it cost much, I wonder?"

And she had her wish. The family had the Chinaman's back mended, and a strong rivet put through his neck; he looked as good as new, but he could no longer nod his head.

"You have become proud since your fall broke you to pieces," said Major-general-field-sergeant-commander Billy-goat's-legs. "You have no reason to give yourself such airs. Am I to have her or not?"

The chimney sweep and the little shepherdess looked piteously at the old Chinaman, for they were afraid he might nod; but he was not able: besides, it was so tiresome to be always telling strangers he had a rivet in the back of his neck.

And so the little china people remained together, and were glad of the grandfather's rivet, and continued to love each other till they were broken to pieces.

# THE TRAVELING COMPANION

Poor John was very sad; for his father was so ill, he had no hope of his recovery. John sat alone with the sick man in the little room, and the lamp had nearly burned out, for it was late in the night.

"You have been a good son, John," said the sick father, "and God will help you on in the world." He looked at him as he spoke, with mild, earnest eyes, drew a deep sigh, and died; yet it appeared as if he still slept.

John wept bitterly. He had no one in the wide world now; neither father, mother, brother, nor sister. Poor John! He knelt down by the bed, kissed his dead father's hand, and wept many, many bitter tears. But at last his eyes closed, and he fell asleep with his head resting against the hard bedpost. Then he dreamed a strange dream; he thought he saw the sun shining upon him, and his father alive and well, and even heard him laughing as he used to do when he was very happy. A beautiful girl, with a golden crown on her head and long, shining hair gave him her hand, and his father said, "See what a bride you have won. She is the loveliest maiden on the whole earth." Then he awoke, and all the beautiful things vanished before his eyes, his father lay dead on the bed, and he was all alone. Poor John!

During the following week the dead man was buried. The son walked behind the coffin which contained his father, whom he so dearly loved, and would never again behold. He heard the earth fall on the coffin lid, and watched it till only a corner remained in sight, and at last that also disappeared. He felt as if his heart would break with the weight of his sorrow, till those who stood around the grave sang a psalm, and the sweet, holy tones brought tears into his eyes, which relieved him.

The sun shone brightly down on the green trees, as if it would say, "You must not be so sorrowful, John. Do you see the beautiful blue sky above you? Your father is up there, and he prays to the loving Father of all, that you may do well in the future."

"I will always be good," said John, "and then I shall go to be with my father in heaven. What joy it will be when we see each other again! How much I shall have to relate to him, and how many things he will be able to explain to me of the delights of heaven, and teach me as he once did on earth. Oh, what joy it will be!"

He pictured it all so plainly to himself, that he smiled even while the tears ran down his cheeks.

The little birds in the chestnut trees twittered, "Tweet, tweet"; they were so happy, although they had seen the funeral; but they seemed as if they knew that the dead man was now in heaven, and that he had wings much larger and more beautiful than their own; and he was happy now, because he had been good here on earth, and they were glad of it. John saw them fly away out of the green trees into the wide world, and he longed to fly with them; but first he cut out a large wooden cross, to place on his father's grave; and when he brought it there in the evening, he found the grave decked out with gravel and flowers. Strangers had done this; they who had known the good old father who was now dead, and who had loved him very much.

Early the next morning, John packed up his little bundle of clothes, and placed all his money, which consisted of fifty dollars and a few shillings, in his girdle; with this he determined to try his fortune in the world. But first he went into the churchyard; and, by his father's grave, he offered up a prayer and said, "Farewell."

As he passed through the fields, all the flowers looked fresh and beautiful in the warm sunshine, and nodded in the wind, as if they wished to say, "Welcome to the green wood, where all is fresh and bright."

Then John turned to have one more look at the old church, in which he had been christened in his infancy, and where his father had taken him every Sunday to hear the service and join in singing the psalms. As he looked at the old tower, he espied the ringer standing at one of the narrow openings, with his little pointed red cap on his head, and shading his eyes from the sun with his bent arm. John nodded farewell to him, and the little ringer waved his red cap, laid his hand on his heart, and kissed his hand to him a great many times, to show that he felt kindly towards him, and wished him a prosperous journey.

John continued his journey, and thought of all the wonderful things he should see in the large, beautiful world, till he found himself farther away from home than ever he had been before. He did not even know the names of the places he passed through, and could scarcely understand the language of the people he met, for he was far away, in a strange land. The first night he slept on a haystack, out in the fields, for there was no other bed for him; but it seemed to him so nice and comfortable that even a king need not wish for a better. The field, the brook, the haystack, with the blue sky above, formed a beautiful sleeping room. The green grass, with the little red and white flowers, was the carpet; the elder bushes and the hedges of wild roses looked like garlands on the walls; and for a bath he could have the clear, fresh water of the brook; while the rushes bowed their heads to him, to wish him good morning and good evening. The moon, like a large lamp, hung high up in the blue ceiling, and he had no fear of its setting fire to his curtains. John slept here quite safely all night; and when he awoke, the sun was up, and all the little birds were singing around him, "Good morning, good morning. Are you not up yet?"

It was Sunday, and the bells were ringing for church. As the people went in, John followed them; he heard God's word, joined in singing the psalms, and listened to the preacher. It seemed to him just as if he were in his own church, where he had been christened, and had sung the psalms with his father. Out in the churchyard were several graves, and on some of them the grass had grown very high. John thought of his father's grave, which he knew at last would look like these, as he was not there to weed and attend to it. Then he set to work, pulled up the high grass, raised the wooden crosses which had fallen down, and replaced the wreaths which had been blown away from their places by the wind, thinking all the time, "Perhaps someone is doing the same for my father's grave, as I am not there to do it."

Outside the church door stood an old beggar, leaning on his crutch. John gave him his silver shillings, and then he continued his journey, feeling lighter and happier than ever. Towards evening, the weather became very stormy, and he hastened on as quickly as he could to get shelter; but it was quite dark by the time he reached a little lonely church which stood on a hill.

"I will go in here," he said, "and sit down in a corner; for I am quite tired, and want rest."

So he went in, and seated himself; then he folded his hands and offered up his evening prayer, and was soon fast asleep and dreaming, while the thunder rolled and the lightning flashed without. When he awoke, it was still night; but the storm had ceased, and the moon shone in upon him through the windows. Then he saw an open coffin standing in the center of the church, which contained a dead man, waiting for burial. John was not at all timid; he had a good conscience, and he knew also that the dead can never injure anyone. It is living wicked men who do harm to others. Two such wicked persons stood now by the dead man, who had been brought to the church to be buried. Their evil intentions were to throw the poor dead body outside the church door, and not leave him to rest in his coffin.

"Why do you do this?" asked John, when he saw what they were going to do. "It is very wicked. Leave him to rest in peace, in Christ's name."

"Nonsense," replied the two dreadful men. "He has cheated us; he owed us money which he could not pay, and now he is dead we shall not get a penny; so we mean to have our revenge, and let him lie like a dog outside the church door."

"I have only fifty dollars," said John, "it is all I possess in the world, but I will give it to you if you will promise me faithfully to leave the dead man in peace. I shall be able to get on without the money; I have strong and healthy limbs, and God will always help me."

"Why, of course," said the horrid men, "if you will pay his debt we will both promise not to touch him. You may depend upon that!" And then they took the money he offered them, laughed at him for his good nature, and went their way.

Then he laid the dead body back in the coffin, folded the hands, and took leave of it; and went away contentedly through the great forest. All around him he could see the prettiest little elves dancing in the moonlight, which shone through the trees. They were not disturbed by his appearance, for they knew he was good and harmless. They are wicked people only who can never obtain a glimpse of fairies. Some of them were not taller than the breadth of a finger, and they wore golden combs in their long, yellow hair. They were rocking themselves two together on the large dewdrops with which the leaves and the high grass were sprinkled. Sometimes the dewdrops would roll away, and then they fell down between the stems of the long grass, and caused a great deal of laughing and noise among the other little people. It was quite charming to watch them at play. Then they sang songs, and John remembered that he had learned those pretty songs when he was a little boy. Large speckled spiders, with silver crowns on their heads, were employed to spin suspension bridges and palaces from one hedge to another, and when the tiny drops fell upon them, they glittered in the moonlight like shining glass. This continued till sunrise. Then the little elves crept into the flower-buds, and the wind seized the bridges and palaces, and fluttered them in the air like cobwebs.

232

As John left the wood, a strong man's voice called after him, "Hallo, comrade, where are you traveling?"

"Into the wide world," he replied; "I am only a poor lad, I have neither father nor mother, but God will help me."

"I am going into the wide world also," replied the stranger. "Shall we keep each other company?"

"With all my heart," he said, and so they went on together.

Soon they began to like each other very much, for they were both good; but John found out that the stranger was much cleverer than himself. He had traveled all over the world, and could describe almost everything.

The sun was high in the heavens when they seated themselves under a large tree to eat their breakfast, and at the same moment an old woman came towards them. She was very old and almost bent double. She leaned upon a stick and carried on her back a bundle of firewood, which she had collected in the forest; her apron was tied around it, and John saw three great stems of fern and some willow twigs peeping out. Just as she came close up to them, her foot slipped and she fell to the ground screaming loudly; poor old woman, she had broken her leg! John proposed directly that they should carry the old woman home to her cottage; but the stranger opened his knapsack and took out a box, in which he said he had a salve that would quickly make her leg well and strong again, so that she would be able to walk home herself, as if her leg had never been broken. And all that he would ask in return was the three fern stems which she carried in her apron.

"That is rather too high a price," said the old woman, nodding her head quite strangely. She did not seem at all inclined to part with the fern stems. However, it was not very agreeable to lie there with a broken leg, so she gave them to him; and such was the power of the ointment, that no sooner had he rubbed her leg with it than the old mother rose up and walked even better than she had done before. But then this wonderful ointment could not be bought at a chemist's.

"What can you want with those three fern rods?" asked John of his fellow traveler.

"Oh, they will make capital brooms," said he; "and I like them because I have strange whims sometimes." Then they walked on together for a long distance.

"How dark the sky is becoming," said John; "and look at those thick, heavy clouds."

"Those are not clouds," replied his fellow traveler; "they are mountains—large lofty mountains—on the tops of which we should be above the clouds, in the pure, free air. Believe me, it is delightful to ascend so high; tomorrow we shall be there."

But the mountains were not so near as they appeared; they had to travel a whole day before they reached them, and pass through black forests and piles of rocks as large as a town. The journey had been so fatiguing that John and his fellow traveler stopped to rest at a roadside inn, so that they might gain strength for their journey on the morrow. In the large public room of the inn a great many persons were assembled to see a comedy performed by dolls. The showman had just erected his little theater, and the people were sitting around the room to witness the performance. Right in front, in the very best place, sat a stout butcher, with a great bulldog by his side who seemed very much inclined to bite. He sat staring with all his eyes, and so indeed did everyone else in the room.

And then the play began. It was a pretty piece, with a king and a queen in it, who sat on a beautiful throne, and had gold crowns on their heads. The trains to their dresses were very long, according to the fashion; while the prettiest of wooden dolls, with glass eyes and large mustaches, stood at the doors, and opened and shut them, that the fresh air might come into the room. It was a very pleasant play, not at all mournful; but just as the queen stood up and walked across the stage, the great bulldog, who should have been held back by his master, made a spring forward, and caught the queen in the teeth by the slender wrist, so that it snapped in two. This was a very dreadful disaster. The poor man who was exhibiting the dolls was much annoyed, and quite sad about his queen; she was the prettiest doll he had, and the bulldog had broken her head and shoulders off.

But after all the people were gone away, the stranger, who came with John, said that he could soon set her to rights. And then he brought out his box and rubbed the doll with some of the salve with which he had cured the old woman when she broke her leg. As soon as this was done, the doll's back became quite right again; her head and shoulders were fixed on, and she could even move her limbs herself: there was now no occasion to pull the wires, for the doll acted just like a living creature, excepting that she could not speak. The man to whom the show belonged was quite delighted at having a doll who could dance of herself without being pulled by the wires; none of the other dolls could do this.

During the night, when all the people at the inn were gone to bed, someone was heard to sigh so deeply and painfully, and the sighing continued for so long a time that everyone got up to see what could be the matter. The showman went at once to his little theater and found that it proceeded from the dolls, who all lay on the floor sighing piteously, and staring with their glass eyes; they all wanted to be rubbed with the ointment, so that, like the queen, they might be able to move of themselves. The queen threw herself on her knees, took off her beautiful crown, and, holding it in her hand, cried, "Take this from me, but do rub my husband and his courtiers."

The poor man who owned the theater could scarcely refrain from weeping; he was so sorry that he could not help them. Then he immediately spoke to John's comrade, and promised him all the money he might receive at the next evening's performance, if he would only rub the ointment on four or five of his dolls. But the fellow traveler said he did not require anything in return, excepting the sword which the showman wore by his side. As soon as he received the sword he anointed six of the dolls with the ointment, and they were able immediately to dance so gracefully that all the living girls in the room could not help joining in the dance. The coachman danced with the cook, and the waiters with the chambermaids, and all the strangers joined; even the tongs and the fire shovel made an attempt, but they fell down after the first jump. So after all it was a very merry night. The next morning John and his companion left the inn to continue their journey through the great pine forests and over the high mountains. They arrived at last at such a great height that towns and villages lay beneath them, and the church steeples looked like little specks between the green trees. They could see for miles around, far away to places they had never visited, and John saw more of the beautiful world than he had ever known before. The sun shone brightly in the blue firmament above, and through the clear mountain air came the sound of the huntsman's horn, and the soft, sweet notes brought tears into his eyes, and he could not help exclaiming, "How good and loving God is to give us all this beauty and loveliness in the world to make us happy!"

His fellow traveler stood by with folded hands, gazing on the dark wood and the towns bathed in the warm sunshine. At this moment there sounded over their heads sweet music. They looked up and discovered a large white swan hovering in the air and singing as no bird had sang before. But the song soon became weaker and weaker, the bird's head drooped, and he sunk slowly down, and lay dead at their feet.

"It is a beautiful bird," said the traveler, "and these large white wings are worth a great deal of money. I will take them with me. You see now that a sword will be very useful."

So he cut off the wings of the dead swan with one blow, and carried them away with him.

They now continued their journey over the mountains for many miles, till they at length reached a large city, containing hundreds of towers, that shone in the sunshine like silver. In the midst of the city stood a splendid marble palace, roofed with pure red gold, in which dwelt the king. John and his companion would not go into the town immediately; so they stopped at an inn outside the town to change their clothes; for they wished to appear respectable as they walked through the streets. The landlord told them that the king was a very good man, who never injured anyone: but as to his daughter, "Heaven defend us!"

She was indeed a wicked princess. She possessed beauty enough—nobody could be more elegant or prettier than she was; but what of that? For she was a wicked witch; and in consequence of her conduct many noble young princes had lost their lives. Anyone was at liberty to make her an offer; were he a prince or a beggar, it mattered not to her. She would ask him to guess three things which she had just thought of, and if he succeed, he was to marry her, and be king over all the land when her father died; but if he could not guess these three things, then she ordered him to be hanged or to have his head cut off.

The old king, her father, was very much grieved at her conduct, but he could not prevent her from being so wicked, because he once said he would have nothing more to do with her lovers; she might do as she pleased. Each prince who came and tried the three guesses, so that he might marry the princess, had been unable to find them out, and had been hanged or beheaded. They had all been warned in time, and might have left her alone, if they would. The old king became at last so distressed at all these dreadful circumstances, that for a whole day every year he and his soldiers knelt and prayed that the princess might become good; but she continued as wicked as ever. The old women who drank brandy would color it quite black before they drank it, to show how they mourned; and what more could they do?

"What a horrible princess!" said John. "She ought to be well flogged. If I were the old king, I would have her punished in some way."

Just then they heard the people outside shouting, "Hurrah!" and, looking out, they saw the princess passing by; and she was really so beautiful that everybody forgot her wickedness, and shouted "Hurrah!" Twelve lovely maidens in white silk dresses, holding golden tulips in their hands, rode by her side on coal-black horses. The princess herself had a snow-white steed, decked with diamonds and rubies. Her dress was of cloth of gold, and the whip she held in her hand looked like a sunbeam. The golden crown on her head glittered like the stars of heaven, and her mantle was formed of thousands of butterflies' wings sewn together. Yet she herself was more beautiful than all.

When John saw her, his face became as red as a drop of blood, and he could scarcely utter a word. The princess looked exactly like the beautiful lady with the golden crown, of whom he had dreamed on the night his father died. She appeared to him so lovely that he could not help loving her.

"It could not be true," he thought, "that she was really a wicked witch, who ordered people to be hanged or beheaded if they could not guess her thoughts. Everyone has permission to go and ask her hand, even the poorest beggar. I shall pay a visit to the palace," he said; "I must go, for I cannot help myself."

Then they all advised him not to attempt it; for he would be sure to share the same fate as the rest. His fellow traveler also tried to persuade him against it; but John seemed quite sure of success. He brushed his shoes and his coat, washed his face and his hands, combed his soft flaxen hair, and then went out alone into the town, and walked to the palace.

"Come in," said the king, as John knocked at the door. John opened it, and the old king, in a dressing gown and embroidered slippers, came towards him. He had the crown on his head, carried his scepter in one hand, and the orb in the other. "Wait a bit," said he, and he placed the orb under his arm, so that he could offer the other hand to John; but when he found that John was another suitor, he began to weep so violently, that both the scepter and the orb fell to the floor, and he was obliged to wipe his eyes with his dressing gown. Poor old king! "Let her alone," he said; "you will fare as badly as all the others. Come, I will show you." Then he led him out into the princess's pleasure gardens, and there he saw a frightful sight. On every tree hung three or four king's sons who had wooed the princess, but had not been able to guess the riddles she gave them. Their skeletons rattled in every breeze, so that the terrified birds never dared to venture into the garden. All the flowers were supported by human bones instead of sticks, and human skulls in the flowerpots grinned horribly. It was really a doleful garden for a princess. "Do you see all this?" said the old king. "Your fate will be the same as those who are here, therefore do not attempt it. You really make me very unhappy—I take these things to heart so very much."

John kissed the good old king's hand, and said he was sure it would be all right, for he was quite enchanted with the beautiful princess. Then the princess herself came riding into the palace yard with all her ladies, and he wished her "Good morning." She looked wonderfully fair and lovely when she offered her hand to John, and he loved her more than ever. How could she be a wicked witch, as all the people asserted?

He accompanied her into the hall, and the little pages offered them gingerbread nuts and sweetmeats, but the old king was so unhappy he could eat nothing, and besides, gingerbread nuts were too hard for him. It was decided that John should come to the palace the next day, when the judges and the whole of the counselors would be present, to try if he could guess the first riddle. If he succeeded, he would have to come a second time; but if not, he would lose his life—and no one had ever been able to guess even one.

However, John was not at all anxious about the result of his trial; on the contrary, he was very merry. He thought only of the beautiful princess, and believed that in some way he should have help, but how he knew not, and did not like to think about it; so he danced along the high road as he went back to the inn, where he had left his fellow traveler waiting for him. John could not refrain from telling him how gracious the princess had been, and how beautiful she looked. He longed for the next day so much, that he might go to the palace and try his luck at guessing the riddles.

But his comrade shook his head, and looked very mournful. "I do so wish you to do well," said he; "we might have continued together much longer, and now I am likely to lose you; you poor dear John! I could shed tears, but I will not make you unhappy on the last night we may be together. We will be merry, really merry this evening; tomorrow, after you are gone, I shall be able to weep undisturbed."

It was very quickly known among the inhabitants of the town that another suitor had arrived for the princess, and there was great sorrow in consequence. The theater remained closed, the women who sold sweetmeats tied crepe around the sugar sticks, and the king and the priests were on their knees in the church. There was a great lamentation, for no one expected John to succeed better than those who had been suitors before.

In the evening John's comrade prepared a large bowl of punch, and said, "Now let us be merry, and drink to the health of the princess." But after drinking two glasses, John became so sleepy that he could not keep his eyes open, and fell fast asleep. Then his fellow traveler lifted him gently out of his chair, and laid him on the bed; and as soon as it was quite dark, he took the two large wings which he had cut from the dead swan, and tied them firmly to his own shoulders. Then he put into his pocket the largest of the three rods which he had obtained from the old woman who had fallen and broken her leg. After this he opened the window and flew away over the town, straight towards the palace, and seated himself in a corner, under the window which looked into the bedroom of the princess.

The town was perfectly still when the clocks struck a quarter to twelve. Presently the window opened, and the princess, who had large black wings to her shoulders, and a long white mantle, flew away over the city towards a high mountain. The fellow traveler, who had made himself invisible so that she could not possibly see him, flew after her through the air, and whipped the princess with his rod, so that blood came whenever he struck her. Ah, it was a strange flight through the air! The wind caught her mantle, so that it spread out on all sides, like the large sail of a ship, and the moon shone through it. "How it hails, to be sure!" said the princess, at each blow she received from the rod; and it served her right to be whipped.

At last she reached the side of the mountain, and knocked. The mountain opened with a noise like the roll of thunder, and the princess went in. The traveler followed her; no one could see him, as he had made himself invisible. They went through a long, wide passage. A thousand gleaming spiders ran here and there on the walls, causing them to glitter as if they were illuminated with fire. They next entered a large hall built of silver and gold. Large red and blue flowers shone on the walls, looking like sunflowers in size, but no one could dare to pluck them, for the stems were hideous poisonous snakes, and the flowers were flames of fire, darting out of their jaws. Shining glowworms covered the ceiling, and sky-blue bats flapped their transparent wings.

Altogether the place had a frightful appearance. In the middle of the floor stood a throne supported by four skeleton horses, whose harness had been made by fiery-red spiders. The throne itself was made of milk-white glass, and the cushions were little black mice, each biting the other's tail. Over it hung a canopy of rose-colored spider's webs, spotted with the prettiest little green flies, which sparkled like precious stones. On the throne sat an old magician with a crown on his ugly head, and a scepter in his hand. He kissed the princess on the forehead, seated her by his side on the splendid throne, and then the music commenced. Great black grasshoppers played the mouth organ, and the owl struck herself on the body instead of a drum. It was altogether a ridiculous concert. Little black goblins with false lights in their caps danced about the hall; but no one could see the traveler, and he had placed himself just behind the throne where he could see and hear everything. The courtiers who came in afterwards looked noble and grand, but anyone with common sense could see what they really were—only broomsticks, with cabbages for heads. The magician had given them life, and dressed them in embroidered robes. It answered very well, as they were only wanted for show. After there had been a little dancing, the princess told the magician that she had a new suitor, and asked him what she could think of for the suitor to guess when he came to the castle the next morning.

"Listen to what I say," said the magician, "you must choose something very easy, as he will be less likely to guess it then. Think of one of your shoes, he will never imagine it is that. Then cut his head off; and mind you do not forget to bring his eyes with you tomorrow night, that I may eat them."

The princess curtsied low, and said she would not forget the eyes.

The magician then opened the mountain and she flew home again, but the traveler followed and flogged her so much with the rod that she sighed quite deeply about the heavy hailstorm, and made as much haste as she could to get back to her bedroom through the window. The traveler then returned to the inn where John still slept, took off his wings, and laid down on the bed, for he was very tired. Early in the morning John awoke, and when his fellow traveler got up, he said that he had a

*"Think of one of your shoes, he will never imagine it is that."*

very wonderful dream about the princess and her shoe, and he therefore advised John to ask her if she had not thought of her shoe. Of course the traveler knew this from what the magician in the mountain had said.

"I may as well say that as anything," said John. "Perhaps your dream may come true; still I will say farewell, for if I guess wrong I shall never see you again."

Then they embraced each other, and John went into the town and walked to the palace. The great hall was full of people, and the judges sat in armchairs, with eiderdown cushions to rest their heads upon, because they had so much to think of. The old king stood near, wiping his eyes with his white pocket handkerchief. When the princess entered, she looked even more beautiful than she had appeared the day before, and greeted everyone present most gracefully; but to John she gave her hand, and said, "Good morning to you."

Now came the time for John to guess what she was thinking of; and oh, how kindly she looked at him as she spoke. But when he uttered the single word "shoe," she turned as pale as a ghost; all her wisdom could not help her, for he had guessed rightly. Oh, how pleased the old king was! It was quite amusing to see how he capered about. All the people clapped their hands, both on his account and John's, who had guessed rightly the first time. His fellow traveler was glad also, when he heard how successful John had been. But John folded his hands and thanked God, who, he felt quite sure, would help him again; and he knew he had to guess twice more.

The evening passed pleasantly like the one preceding. While John slept, his companion flew behind the princess to the mountain, and flogged her even harder than before; this time he had taken two rods with him. No one saw him go in with her, and he heard all that was said. The princess this time was to think of a glove, and he told John as if he had again heard it in a dream. The next day, therefore, he was able to guess correctly the second time, and it caused great rejoicing at the palace. The whole court jumped about as they had seen the king do the day before, but the princess lay on the sofa, and would not say a single word. All now depended upon John. If he only guessed rightly the third time, he would marry the princess, and reign over the kingdom after the death of the old king: but if he failed, he would lose his life, and the magician would have his beautiful blue eyes.

That evening John said his prayers and went to bed very early, and soon fell asleep calmly. But his companion tied on his wings to his shoulders, took three rods, and, with his sword at his side, flew to the palace. It was a very dark night, and so stormy that the tiles flew from the roofs of the houses, and the trees in the garden upon which the skeletons hung bent themselves like reeds before the wind. The lightning flashed, and the thunder rolled in one long-continued peal all night. The window of the castle opened, and the princess flew out. She was pale as death, but she laughed at the storm as if it were not bad enough. Her white mantle fluttered in the wind like a large sail, and the traveler flogged her with the three rods till the blood trickled down, and at last she could scarcely fly; she contrived, however, to reach the mountain. "What a hailstorm!" she said, as she entered; "I have never been out in such weather as this."

"Yes, there may be too much of a good thing sometimes," said the magician.

Then the princess told him that John had guessed rightly the second time, and if he succeeded the next morning, he would win, and she could never come to the mountain again, or practice magic as she had done, and therefore she was quite unhappy. "I will find out something for you to think of which he will never guess, unless he is a greater conjuror than myself. But now let us be merry."

Then he took the princess by both hands, and they danced with all the little goblins and jack-o'-lanterns in the room. The red spiders sprang here and there on the walls quite as merrily, and the flowers of fire appeared as if they were throwing out sparks. The owl beat the drum, the crickets whistled, and the grasshoppers played the mouth organ. It was a very ridiculous ball. After they had danced enough, the princess was obliged to go home, for fear she should be missed at the palace. The magician offered to go with her, that they might be company to each other on the way. Then they flew away through the bad weather, and the traveler followed them, and broke his three rods across their shoulders. The magician had never been out in such a hailstorm as this. Just by the palace the magician stopped to wish the princess farewell, and to whisper in her ear, "Tomorrow, think of my head."

But the traveler heard it, and just as the princess slipped through the window into her bedroom, and the magician turned around to fly back to the mountain, he seized him by the long black beard, and with his saber cut off the wicked conjuror's head just behind the shoulders, so that he could not even see who it was. He threw the body into the sea to the fishes, and after dipping the head into the water, he tied it up in a silk handkerchief, took it with him to the inn, and then went to bed. The next morning he gave John the handkerchief, and told him not to untie it till the princess asked him what she was thinking of. There were so many people in the great hall of the palace that they stood as thick as radishes tied together in a bundle. The council sat in their armchairs with the white cushions. The old king wore new robes, and the golden crown and scepter had been polished up so that he looked quite smart. But the princess was very pale, and wore a black dress as if she were going to a funeral.

"What have I thought of?" asked the princess of John. He immediately untied the handkerchief, and was himself quite frightened when he saw the head of the ugly magician. Everyone shuddered, for it was terrible to look at; but the princess sat like a statue, and could not utter a single word. At length she rose and gave John her hand, for he had guessed rightly.

She looked at no one, but sighed deeply, and said, "You are my master now; this evening our marriage must take place."

"I am very pleased to hear it," said the king. "It is just what I wish."

Then all the people shouted "Hurrah." The band played music in the streets, the bells rang, and the cake women took the black crepe off the sugar sticks. There was universal joy. Three oxen, stuffed with ducks and chickens, were roasted whole in the marketplace, where everyone might help himself to a slice. The fountains spouted forth the most delicious wine, and whoever bought a penny loaf at the baker's received six large buns, full of raisins, as a present. In the evening the whole town was illuminated. The soldiers fired off cannons, and the boys let off crackers. There was eating and drinking, dancing and jumping everywhere. In the palace, the high-born gentlemen and beautiful ladies danced with each other, and they could be heard at a great distance singing the following song:

> *"Here are maidens, young and fair,*
> *Dancing in the summer air;*
> *Like two spinning wheels at play,*
> *Pretty maidens dance away—*
> *Dance the spring and summer through*
> *Till the sole falls from your shoe."*

But the princess was still a witch, and she could not love John. His fellow traveler had thought of that, so he gave John three feathers out of the swan's wings, and a little bottle with a few drops in it. He told him to place a large bath full of water by the princess's bed, and put the feathers and the drops into it. Then, at the moment she was about to get into bed, he must give her a little push, so that she might fall into the water, and then dip her three times. This would destroy the power of the magician, and she would love him very much. John did all that his companion told him to do. The princess shrieked aloud when he dipped her under the water the first time, and struggled under his hands in the form of a great black swan with fiery eyes. As she rose the second time from the water, the swan had become white, with a black ring around its neck. John allowed the water to close once more over the bird, and at the same time it changed into a most beautiful princess. She was more lovely even than before, and thanked him, while her eyes sparkled with tears, for having broken the spell of the magician.

The next day, the king came with the whole court to offer their congratulations, and stayed till quite late. Last of all came the traveling companion; he had his staff in his hand and his knapsack on his back. John kissed him many times and told him that he must not go—that he must remain with him, for he was the cause of all his good fortune. But the traveler shook his head, and said gently and kindly, "No: my time is up now; I have only paid my debt to you. Do you remember the dead man whom the bad people wished to throw out of his coffin? You gave all you possessed that he might rest in his grave; I am that man." As he said this, he vanished.

The wedding festivities lasted a whole month. John and his princess loved each other dearly, and the old king lived to see many a happy day, when he took their little children on his knees and let them play with his scepter. And John became king over the whole country.

# THE ELFIN HILL

A few large lizards were running nimbly about in the clefts of an old tree; they could understand one another very well, for they spoke the lizard language.

"What a buzzing and a rumbling there is in the elfin hill," said one of the lizards; "I have not been able to close my eyes for two nights on account of the noise; I might just as well have had the toothache, for that always keeps me awake."

"There is something going on within there," said the other lizard; "they propped up the top of the hill with four red posts, till cock-crow this morning, so that it is thoroughly aired, and the elfin girls have learned new dances; there is something."

"I spoke about it to an earthworm of my acquaintance," said a third lizard; "the earthworm had just come from the elfin hill, where he has been groping about in the earth day and night. He has heard a great deal; although he cannot see, poor miserable creature, yet he understands very well how to wriggle and lurk about. They expect friends in the elfin hill, grand company, too; but who they are the earthworm would not say, or, perhaps, he really did not know. All the will-o'-the-wisps are ordered to be there to hold a torch dance, as it is called. The silver and gold which is plentiful in the hill will be polished and placed out in the moonlight."

"Who can the strangers be?" asked the lizards. "What can the matter be? Hark, what a buzzing and humming there is!"

Just at this moment the elfin hill opened, and an old elfin maiden, hollow in the back, came tripping out; she was the old elf king's housekeeper, and a distant relative of the family; therefore she wore an amber heart on the middle of her forehead. Her feet moved very fast, "trip, trip"; good gracious, how she could trip right down to the sea to the night raven.

"You are invited to the elf hill for this evening," said she; "but will you do me a great favor and undertake the invitations? You ought to do something, for you have no housekeeping to attend to as I have. We are going to have some very grand people, conjurors, who have always something to say; and therefore the old elf king wishes to make a great display."

"Who is to be invited?" asked the raven.

*They danced in shawls woven from moonshine and mist.*

"All the world may come to the great ball, even human beings, if they can only talk in their sleep, or do something after our fashion. But for the feast the company must be carefully selected; we can only admit persons of high rank; I have had a dispute myself with the elf king, as he thought we could not admit ghosts. The merman and his daughter must be invited first, although it may not be agreeable to them to remain so long on dry land, but they shall have a wet stone to sit on, or perhaps something better; so I think they will not refuse this time. We must have all the old demons of the first class, with tails, and the hobgoblins and imps; and then I think we ought not to leave out the death horse, or the grave pig, or even the church dwarf, although they do belong to the clergy, and are not reckoned among our people; but that is merely their office, they are nearly related to us, and visit us very frequently."

"Croak," said the night raven as he flew away with the invitations.

The elfin maidens were already dancing on the elf hill, and they danced in shawls woven from moonshine and mist, which look very pretty to those who like such things. The large hall within the elf hill was splendidly decorated; the floor had been washed with moonshine, and the walls had been rubbed with magic ointment, so that they glowed like tulip leaves in the light. In the kitchen were frogs roasting on the spit, and dishes preparing of snail skins, with children's fingers in them, salad of mushroom seed, hemlock, noses and marrow of mice, beer from the marsh woman's brewery, and sparkling saltpeter wine from the grave cellars. These were all substantial food. Rusty nails and church-window glass formed the dessert. The old elf king had his gold crown polished up with powdered slate pencil; it was like that used by the first form, and very difficult for an elf king to obtain. In the bedrooms, curtains were hung up and fastened with the slime of snails; there was, indeed, a buzzing and humming everywhere.

"Now we must fumigate the place with burned horsehair and pig's bristles, and then I think I shall have done my part," said the elf manservant.

"Father, dear," said the youngest daughter, "may I now hear who our high-born visitors are?"

"Well, I suppose I must tell you now," he replied; "two of my daughters must prepare themselves to be married, for the marriages certainly will take place. The old goblin from Norway, who lives in the ancient Dovre mountains, and who possesses many castles built of rock and freestone, besides a gold mine, which is better than all, so it is thought, is coming with his two sons, who are both seeking a wife. The old goblin is a true-hearted, honest, old Norwegian graybeard; cheerful and straightforward. I knew him formerly, when we used to drink together to our good fellowship: he came here once to fetch his wife, who is dead now. She was the daughter of the king of the chalk hills at Moen. They say he took his wife from chalk; I shall be delighted to see him again. It is said that the boys are ill-bred, forward lads, but perhaps that is not quite correct, and they will become better as they grow older. Let me see that you know how to teach them good manners."

"And when are they coming?" asked the daughter.

"That depends upon wind and weather," said the elf king; "they travel economically. They will come when there is the chance of a ship. I wanted them to come over to Sweden, but the old man was not inclined to take my advice. He does not go forward with the times, and that I do not like."

Two will-o'-the-wisps came jumping in, one quicker than the other, so of course, one arrived first.

"They're coming! They're coming!" he cried.

"Give me my crown," said the elf king, "and let me stand in the moonshine."

The daughters drew on their shawls and bowed down to the ground. There stood the old goblin from the Dovre mountains, with his crown of hardened ice and polished fir cones. Besides this, he wore a bearskin and great, warm boots, while his sons went with their throats bare and wore no braces, for they were strong men.

"Is that a hill?" said the youngest of the boys, pointing to the elf hill. "We should call it a hole in Norway."

"Boys," said the old man, "a hole goes in, and a hill stands out; have you no eyes in your heads?"

Another thing they wondered at was that they were able without trouble to understand the language.

"Take care," said the old man, "or people will think you have not been well brought up."

Then they entered the elfin hill, where the select and grand company were assembled, and so quickly had they appeared that they seemed to have been blown together. But for each guest the neatest and pleasantest arrangement had been made. The sea folks sat at the table in great water tubs, and they said it was just like being at home.

*They entered the elfin hill, where the select and grand company were assembled.*

All behaved themselves properly excepting the two young northern goblins; they put their legs on the table and thought they were all right.

"Feet off the tablecloth!" said the old goblin. They obeyed, but not immediately. Then they tickled the ladies who waited at the table with the fir cones, which they carried in their pockets. They took off their boots, that they might be more at ease, and gave them to the ladies to hold.

But their father, the old goblin, was very different; he talked pleasantly about the stately Norwegian rocks, and told fine tales of the waterfalls which dashed over them with a clattering noise like thunder or the sound of an organ, spreading their white foam on every side. He told of the salmon that leaps in the rushing waters, while the water god plays on his golden harp. He spoke of the bright winter nights, when the sled bells are ringing, and the boys run with burning torches across the smooth ice, which is so transparent that they can see the fishes dart forward beneath their feet. He described everything so clearly, that those who listened could see it all; they could see the sawmills going, the menservants and the maidens singing songs and dancing a rattling dance—when all at once the old goblin gave the old elfin maiden a kiss, such a tremendous kiss, and yet they were almost strangers to each other.

Then the elfin girls had to dance, first in the usual way, and then with stamping feet, which they performed very well; then followed the artistic and solo dance. Dear me, how they did throw their legs about! No one could tell where the dance begun, or where it ended, nor indeed which were legs and which were arms, for they were all flying about together, like the shavings in a saw pit! And then they spun around so quickly that the death horse and the grave pig became sick and giddy, and were obliged to leave the table.

"Stop!" cried the old goblin. "Is that the only housekeeping they can perform? Can they do anything more than dance and throw about their legs, and make a whirlwind?"

"You shall soon see what they can do," said the elf king. And then he called his youngest daughter to him. She was slender and fair as moonlight, and the most graceful of all the sisters. She took a white chip in her mouth, and vanished instantly; this was her accomplishment. But the old goblin said he should not like his wife to have such an accomplishment, and thought his boys would have the same objection. Another daughter could make a figure like herself follow her, as if she had a shadow, which none of the goblin folk ever had. The third was of quite a different sort; she had learned in the brew house of the moor witch how to lard elfin puddings with glowworms.

"She will make a good housewife," said the old goblin, and then saluted her with his eyes instead of drinking her health; for he did not drink much.

Now came the fourth daughter, with a large harp to play upon; and when she struck the first chord, everyone lifted up the left leg (for the goblins are left-legged), and at the second chord they found they must all do just what she wanted.

"That is a dangerous woman," said the old goblin; and the two sons walked out of the hill; they had had enough of it. "And what can the next daughter do?" asked the old goblin.

"I have learned everything that is Norwegian," said she; "and I will never marry, unless I can go to Norway."

Then her youngest sister whispered to the old goblin, "That is only because she has heard, in a Norwegian song, that when the world shall decay, the cliffs of Norway will remain standing like monuments; and she wants to get there, that she may be safe; for she is so afraid of sinking."

"Ho! Ho!" said the old goblin. "Is that what she means? Well, what can the seventh and last do?"

"The sixth comes before the seventh," said the elf king, for he could reckon; but the sixth would not come forward.

"I can only tell people the truth," said she. "No one cares for me, nor troubles himself about me; and I have enough to do to sew my grave clothes."

So the seventh and last came; and what could she do? Why, she could tell stories, as many as you liked, on any subject.

"Here are my five fingers," said the old goblin; "now tell me a story for each of them."

So she took him by the wrist, and he laughed till he nearly choked; and when she came to the fourth finger, there was a gold ring on it, as if it knew there was to be a betrothal. Then the old goblin said, "Hold fast what you have: this hand is yours; for I will have you for a wife myself."

Then the elfin girl said that the stories about the ring finger and little Peter Playman had not yet been told.

"We will hear them in the winter," said the old goblin, "and also about the fir and the birch trees, and the ghost stories, and of the tingling frost. You shall tell your tales, for no one over there can do it so well; and we will sit in the stone rooms, where the pine logs are burning, and drink mead out of the golden drinking horn of the old Norwegian kings. The water god has given me two; and when we sit there, Nix comes to pay us a visit, and will sing you all the songs of the mountain shepherdesses. How merry we shall be! The salmon will be leaping in the waterfalls, and dashing against the stone walls, but he will not be able to come in. It is indeed very pleasant to live in old Norway. But where are the lads?"

Where indeed were they? Why, running about the fields, and blowing out the will-o'-the-wisps, who so good-naturedly came and brought their torches.

"What tricks have you been playing?" said the old goblin. "I have taken a mother for you, and now you may take one of your aunts."

But the youngsters said they would rather make a speech and drink to their good fellowship; they had no wish to marry. Then they made speeches and drank toasts, and tipped their glasses, to show that they were empty. Then they took off their coats, and lay down on the table to sleep; for they made themselves quite at home. But the old goblin danced about the room with his young bride, and exchanged boots with her, which is more fashionable than exchanging rings.

"The cock is crowing," said the old elfin maiden who acted as housekeeper; "now we must close the shutters, that the sun may not scorch us."

Then the hill closed up. But the lizards continued to run up and down the riven tree; and one said to the other, "Oh, how much I was pleased with the old goblin!"

"The boys pleased me better," said the earthworm. But then the poor miserable creature could not see.